PENGUIN BOOKS

SCHOOM

Jonathan Wilson was born in London in 1950. He was educated at the Universities of Essex, Oxford, and the Hebrew University of Jerusalem. His first novel, *The Hiding Room*, will be published by Viking in August 1995. He lives in Newton, Massachusetts with his wife and two sons.

Jonathan Wilson

SCHOOM

PENGUIN BOOKS

For Sharon and for Adam and Gabriel

PENGUIN BOOKS
Published by the Penguin Group
Penguin Books USA Inc., 375 Hudson Street, New York, New York 10014, U.S.A.
Penguin Books Ltd, 27 Wrights Lane, London W8 5TZ, England
Penguin Books Australia Ltd, Ringwood, Victoria, Australia
Penguin Books Canada Ltd, 10 Alcorn Avenue, Toronto, Ontario, Canada M4V 3B2
Penguin Books (N.Z.) Ltd, 182–190 Wairau Road, Auckland 10, New Zealand

Penguin Books Ltd, Registered Offices: Harmondsworth, Middlesex, England

First published in Great Britain by Lime Tree,
an imprint of Reed Consumer Books Ltd 1993
Published in Penguin Books 1995

10 9 8 7 6 5 4 3 2 1

Wilson

"Schoom" and "Charcoal on Paper" first appeared in slightly different form in
Tikkun and "Gathering Rosie" in *The New Yorker*.

PUBLISHER'S NOTE
These selections are works of fiction. Names, characters, places, and incidents either are
the product of the author's imagination or are used fictitiously, and any resemblance
to actual persons, living or dead, events, or locales is entirely coincidental.

LIBRARY OF CONGRESS CATALOGING IN PUBLICATION DATA
Wilson, Jonathan, 1950–
Schoom/Jonathan Wilson.
p.   cm.
Contents: Gathering Rosie—Bank holiday—Savyon—Migrants—From Shanghai—
Schoom—Physically correct—Omaha—Shoes—Paris nights—Charcoal on paper—
Not far from Jericho.
ISBN 0 14 02.3827 1
1. Manners and customs—Fiction.   I. Title.
PR6073.I4679S324   1995
823´.914—dc20   95–1322

Printed in the United States of America
Set in Aldus

Contents

Gathering Rosie

'Tell me something,' said Morris, my father-in-law-to-be. 'What would a guy like you make?'

'A guy like me,' I replied, 'would make about the same as I do.'

We were sitting on my balcony at 3 Bezalel Street, Jerusalem, which is where I lived between the Yom Kippur War and Ariel Sharon's adventure in Lebanon.

'Don't be a wiseguy,' said Morris, 'I don't like wiseguys.'

I was intrigued. I had never had a conversation with a two-fisted American in plaid pants and a pressed white shirt. According to Rosie, Morris had had a fist fight with her previous fiancé. 'He swore at Daddy and Daddy punched him in the mouth.'

'Are both your parents Jewish?' Morris was asking.

'Yes,' I replied, 'from cradle to grave.'

'What's that supposed to mean?'

'It means I live on my salary' (I taught in the local art school) 'and what I can get for my work. My parents are dead. They left nothing.'

'Stone poor,' said Morris, sadly shaking his head, 'and about to marry my daughter.'

I plucked a handful of olives from the high branches of the tree that overhung my terrace. They were small and hard, like the smooth pebbles I could feel rattling inside my head whenever the topic of money came up in my life. 'These need soaking,' I announced, by way of changing the subject. 'In brine.'

Morris gave me a weird look, then relented. 'There used to be a store in London,' he said, 'when I was stationed

there during the war. Brooks's, it was called. The shop
floor was sprinkled with sawdust. They had a barrel full
of sweet and sour pickles, and new green cucumbers. The
sweet and sour were always too soft. I told Brooks. He
threw me out of the store. Me, a young man in uniform.
Can you imagine? But that was all long ago. The question
today is: why do you want to marry my daughter?'

I had to admit, this was the question of questions. I
took a deep breath, then I said, 'Can a man take fire in
his bosom and his clothes not be burned?' In the context
of our conversation, or perhaps any conversation, it was
a stupid thing to say.

'What's that?' Morris asked. 'A line? Are you feeding
me a line, like "Is the Pope Jewish?" ' Luckily, at this
moment, Rosie came out to join us. Her hair was covered
in tinfoil.

'What are you doing,' asked her father, 'roofing your
head?'

'It's to keep the heat in, it makes the colour of the henna
intensify,' Rose replied. She was one of those people who
knew that the best way to defuse an insulting question
was to give a straight answer.

We sat and drank tea suffused with the mint flavour of
nana leaves. The sun, well into its descent behind the
adjacent apartments, was half an orange resting on a concrete block. 'When my mother came from Russia,' Morris
remarked, 'she put a sugar lump in her mouth before she
drank her tea. She drank the tea through the sugar. You
see what I'm saying? My father, on the other hand, put
half a slice of lemon in his tea. Do you know why? Because
it reminded him of a sunset. Warmth. The shape of the
lemon.'

I was bowled over by the arrival of poetry on my balcony in the form of Mr Liverman's anecdote. In appreci-
ation, and wanting to contribute something of my own, I
said, 'Let me show you my cup sculpture.' I had glued a
mug onto the encrusted lid of an old paint can, painted

the piece black and green, and then scratched at it with a nail.

We moved back into my apartment. The three of us squeezed into the area next to the kitchen that I wistfully referred to as 'the studio'. Morris walked round the cup. 'Yes,' he said finally, 'very nice. But what I don't understand about you is this: why do you go on making things if you haven't sold what you've already got? You have a room full of merchandise. If you don't mind my saying so, you have overstock. I see a lot of sculptures here, a helluva lot. Have you thought of reducing the price? Sometimes in these situations a sale is not a bad idea. Lower the price. Empty your warehouse. Begin again.'

'Oh, Dad,' Rose interrupted, coming to my defence, 'It doesn't work like that. This is the creative process, not the fur business.'

'You know what this cup-saucer thing would be nice for?' asked Morris, brushing aside his daughter's distinction with a wave of his hand. 'Pens and pencils. On a desk.'

I went to see Hannah, my ex-shrink, who happens to be a very beautiful woman. In those days she had long hair, almost down to her waist, and a face like Bianca Jagger's. We were supposed to be in a post-therapy friends phase. This was hard because I was used to letting myself go in her company, but now that I was no longer paying her, the expression of wild and excessive feelings was not permitted.

I settled into a brocaded red armchair in her front room (she wouldn't let me near her office). 'Should I marry?' I asked.

'Well,' she replied, 'far be it from me to interfere with your plans.'

'What are you talking about?' I said. 'You're my therapist.'

'Not any more,' she reminded me cruelly. I looked around the room. Her shelves were stuffed with books on death and dying. Outside, on Ramban Street, brakes squealed and the pneumatic doors of an Egged bus folded open and slammed shut. I rambled on for a while about my ambivalence and indecisiveness. Hannah listened intently, occasionally nodding her head. Then, all of a sudden, she rose from her seat. 'You know,' she said, 'I have something for you. I meant to give it to you at our final session, but I forgot.' She moved to a small glass cabinet and took out a scroll tied with pink ribbon. She held it out to me. Had I graduated? Was this a secret thing that everybody got at the end of therapy? A certificate: 'You are slightly less neurotic than you were ten years ago.'

Out on the street, under a night sky dotted with pearly stars, I unrolled my award. It was a small reproduction of a painting by Oskar Kokoschka called *The Tempest*. A man lay alone in a bed, storm-tossed on an ocean. He didn't look too happy.

I decided to walk home instead of taking the bus. ('You don't have a car?' Rosie's father had asked. 'Then how do you get around?') On the corner of Ussishkin Street a man in a leather apron and a green woollen cap was selling flowers. As I passed, he held out a huge bunch of giant yellow chrysanthemums. He looked, for a moment, like the Statue of Liberty. I didn't stop. 'What are you afraid of?' he yelled after me as I wandered up the road. 'Bring a little light into your life.'

Yes. Rosie was light, and I did love her, but marriage? Probably, I had lived alone too long. I was nearly thirty-five. It was time to grow up. My whole life I had been playing around in clay. I stuck things together, then I pulled them apart. Then I put them back together in a different way. This was bad preparation for marriage. Or was it?

I turned in through a trellised entrance-way halfway up the street. My friend Muni had constructed it to raise a grapevine. He had succeeded. After he was done, it turned out that the other families in his apartment building were opposed to grapes. They tore the vine down. The trellis stood as a monument to sweetness and its adversaries.

Muni and Ada's kitchen was in noisy motion: children wriggled around the room, plates spun, stacks of students' exercise books blasted off from one table and crashed down on another. 'Marry?' I yelled above the din. 'Should I marry?' Ada and Muni may have begun to laugh, but who could tell? A cut knee was bandaged, goldfish were fed, a small dog got tangled in my feet and brought me to the ground. I lay supine while four cups of Wissotzky tea rowed very fast from side to side on the edge of the kitchen table that was now my horizon.

'Of course you should marry.' (It was a woman's voice.) 'Misery loves company.' I got up, brushed myself down, and left without anybody noticing.

Outside, in front of the Ussishkin Laundromat, I got caught up in a small crowd pressing to get into the temple next door. I went in too. I hadn't been inside a temple without a good reason (bar mitzvah, wedding, death) for a quarter of a century. Prayers were in progress, some serious bobbing and weaving was going on. Up and down, side to side. Try-outs, I thought; this place is a gym. Someone touched my arm and pointed to my bare head, which I quickly covered. Someone else thrust a book into my hands. I looked around at the sea of white shirts. It was Friday night. By now I should have been back with Rose and her father. But I wasn't ready. My neighbour, a short, bearded man, with a lot of grey hair coming out of his ears, jabbed a finger at a place in my text. With the others I repeated, 'Come, my friend, to meet the bride; let us welcome the presence of the Sabbath.'

After the service I remained in my seat. A blast of warm air hosed down with jasmine came in through the open windows and mingled with the sweat of the departing congregants. A tall, old man with a large face and deep-set eyes slowly came towards me. His bald head and thick nose reminded me of a drawing I had once seen of Cro-Magnon man.

'You're new,' he said, and then added, 'American?'

'No,' I replied, 'English. But I've been here for years. I'm in exile from the world where art crosses paths with commerce.'

He looked at me very carefully, then asked, 'So, apart from that, what's the problem?'

'Who said there was a problem?'

He didn't speak, but drilled his prehistoric fingers on the vinyl-covered seat next to mine. So far this was better than therapy, better than friends.

'The truth is, I'm thinking of getting married.'

There was a long silence. I waited for his ancient wisdom to percolate. Finally, he said, 'Don't be a schmuck, it's groans on groans.' Then he rose, and walked out of the temple.

That's it, I thought, that's enough. Fuck them all. I'm going to get married. I went back to the Statue of Liberty and bought his flaming torch. I walked home through the neighbourhood of Nachlaot, past its tiny, makeshift houses that looked as if they had been thrown together from sheets, towels and cardboard. Each flimsy construction, I was sure, housed a perfectly contented married couple. Right now they were all sharing harmonious Friday-night meals, candles burned on their dinner tables and love in their hearts. Here was an entire neighbourhood of individuals slow to anger and easy to pacify.

Back in my own apartment Morris was standing alone staring out of the window at the city skyline. Rosie was nowhere to be seen. 'Here's a mystery,' said Morris. 'You go in the bathroom, you do your business. You smell nothing. You come out. For some reason – maybe you forgot to brush your teeth or you left your watch on the sink – you go back in. A terrible smell! Who can explain a thing like that? It's like you're two people. The one who's in there, and the one who goes back in. Now, if you go in right after someone else has been in there, a different story, a smell right away.'

What could I say? There are moments in life when we see very clearly. Morris had been granted such a moment. He had been delivered a truth, and in his generosity he had passed it on to me. In return I offered him my chrysanthemum torch. Morris, turning from the window, took the flowers, then looked me straight in the eyes. 'Can I ask you a favour?' he said. 'Live together. Try an experiment. In my opinion Rose is too young to get married. She's on her junior year abroad.'

'No,' I replied, 'that was six years ago. She lives here now. She doesn't even go to school any more. She's a botanist with the Nature Reserve Authority.'

'Time flies,' said Morris, sitting down at my kitchen table. 'One minute a bat mitzvah, the next, your daughter's making a tent out of the sheets with a thirty-five-year-old unemployed man.'

I let this slide. 'We've been living together,' I went on, 'for a year and a half.'

'Look,' Morris continued firmly, 'when Rose's mother was alive, I was harsh. I wanted to have everything my way. Then Tessie got sick, very sick. What could I do about it? You can't force your will on nature. Sometimes you can bend it, like your Uri Geller can bend a spoon, but most of the time not. So what I'm saying to you is this: rent a bigger apartment, I'll pay the extra cost. Live with Rose in a less cramped environment. If you're happy after a year, get married. If not, strike out in separate directions. You take the high road, she takes the low road, or vice versa.'

He hadn't heard a word I'd said. But never mind, his apartment idea was a good one. We did need more space. I didn't think I could take the money (I had *some* pride) but I could accept the proposal.

Rose came banging up the stairs, her arms loaded down with groceries. The henna had given her hair a copper tinge. 'Nice helmet you're wearing,' said her father. 'Where's your shield and lance?'

Rose dumped the bags down onto the kitchen table. A kohlrabi and two tomatoes spilled out and rolled onto the floor.

'Guess what?' I said. 'We're moving. It's your father's idea.'

'Great,' Rose replied, 'nice of you two to make plans on my behalf.' She picked up the vegetables, washed them, and began to slice the kohlrabi. 'Try some of this, Dad.' She held a piece out to her father. 'It's just like radish, only not so sharp.'

Morris made a face. 'Your mother loved radishes. It's an acquired taste.'

'Radishes,' Rose replied, 'are a basic vegetable. There's nothing sophisticated about them.' She was in some mood, no doubt brought on my my take-it-for-granted moving suggestion.

When we were done with supper, Rose made an announcement. 'I have to go to Tel Aviv. I'll be away five or six days. If you want to find us a bigger apartment, that's fine with me, but you and Daddy will have to do it on your own.'

Later, after Morris had gone back to his hotel and we were in bed, I asked, 'Why are you going away?'

'That's my business,' Rose replied. She didn't say it in a nasty way, but even so I felt as if someone had jabbed me in the chest with a sharp object. 'If you're going to marry me,' she went on 'you'll have to get used to my behaviour. You're a middle-aged man with a young girl.' She started to laugh. There's a time to laugh and a time to weep, I thought, as Rose climbed on top of me to get a better view of my face.

So Morris and I wandered the cheap but trendy neighbourhoods of Jerusalem. We roamed the narrow streets down by the railway tracks in Ba'ka, where a garden of junk, a sculptor's delight, had grown up in the space between the fence and the road. I scavenged in this metal graveyard, sorting the discarded cans, auto parts, refrigerator doors and broken boilers, while Morris stood beside me and pondered the apartments we had just visited. 'A top floor, with no proper roof-gutters – a winter nightmare!' 'I'm not sure I like the idea of a shared roof garden. Could be trouble.' 'That place we just saw, in my opinion, and never having lived in Israel you understand, was a slum.' He was generally right, and I appreciated his input. Forty years in the fur business hones certain skills. Morris was direct in his questioning of landlords, deft in his approach to financial matters, alive to rip-offs.

On the fourth day of our search (and of Rosie's absence, no phone calls, no nothing), after a depressing visit to a dingy basement owned by a crabby old woman who kept chickens in her yard ('Picturesque, but not a place to live' – Morris Liverman), I was about ready to give up. Morris was more sanguine. 'When you look for property you can't rush things. Meanwhile, there are intrusions of beauty.'

'What?' I said.

'Look,' he replied, gesturing towards the railway, 'poppies.' He walked over to the embankment and I followed. We stood ankle-deep in a thin, straggly line of wild blood-red flowers. They didn't look like poppies to me, but I couldn't identify what they were. Morris started to whistle a little tune to himself, then fell silent.

'There was a time when you could take the train that passed here all the way to Egypt,' I said, and as I spoke I had a vision of Rose speeding through the desert on the Cairo Express, locked in the arms (and legs!) of some young British officer who knew the names of all the flowers.

'Yes,' Morris replied, 'that was before.'

'They ripped up the rails in the Sinai,' I continued, by way of getting Rose off-track, 'to make the Bar-Lev line.'

'Really,' said Morris, and now he began to whistle in earnest. 'Know what that was?' he asked, pausing for breath. ' "They're going to hang out their washing on the Siegfried line".'

As if we had both decided to free-associate simultaneously, we looked up together towards a line of laundry stretched from the corner of a stone house to a gatepost. Three athletic-style brassières and two pairs of white tights moved gently in the breeze. From our elevated position at the side of the tracks we could see, inscribed in Hebrew and English, a large, hand-painted FOR RENT sign in one of the upper windows of the house.

'This is a *meshugganeh* place,' whispered Morris almost as soon as we had crossed the threshold. The owner, a slight but muscular blonde with a very pretty face (maybe I really *shouldn't* get married, I thought) showed us around and filled us in on the history. Once, she told us, the house had been owned by a Turkish pasha. He had built the place to purdah his unmarried daughters: there were still bars on the windows. Naomi, the present incumbent, was an acrobat. She was off to spend two years in Europe.

Near where Morris was standing a trapeze hung from the ceiling. You could grab it from halfway up the stairs and swing across the room to a landing spot in a window alcove. 'I'll take it,' I said to Naomi. 'High ceilings, a big work space, it's what I need.'

'You want to live in a prison for virgins?' Morris whispered in my ear. 'You think Rose will appreciate this?'

'Oh,' I said, remembering that there was a Rose, 'she'll love it.'

I always hated moving. My muscles tensed up, my nerves frayed. Rose's disappearance only made things worse. I was about halfway through packing our stuff, in fact I was bending to put Rose's diaphragm in the 'bathroom box' (was I glad or distressed that she didn't have it with her?) when I pulled my back out. Agony. It took me five minutes to straighten up, then I discovered that I couldn't bend forward more than an inch.

I called friends. As soon as I mentioned 'packing' everyone was on reserve duty, or at an important meeting in Haifa, or picking up a relative at the airport. Even Muni and Ada were unavailable: they had two sick kids and their car had broken down.

'I don't need a car,' I said, 'Morris loaned me his rental, he told me he'd sit by the pool for a day or two.'

'Oh, Sam' said Ada, 'hire a schlepper, but not one of the Jewish ones, they're all *gruzhinim*, they cheat you. Go to the Old City.'

At midday, under a hot September sun, I approached the shadow of Jaffa gate. A bunch of kids flew by and glued themselves onto a circle of tourists. They offered postcards, tours of the city, sesame bagels, speckled eggs, reedy flutes, drums the size of castanets. I circled the crowd and made for the low wall in front of the Citadel. There I found Ahmed. He was wearing the uniform that had been described to me by Ada: a poncho fashioned out of a length of carpet, and a cummerbund of ropes. I explained my situation. 'You need a truck?' he asked, 'My son has.'

'No,' I replied, 'I need you.' My heart was sinking. Ahmed was sixty if he was a day. He was skinny, Giacometti skinny. At a push, I could think of him as 'wiry'.

'This is what I do,' said Ahmed. He bent forward, almost double, and showed me how he used the small of his back as a pivot. 'A piano, downstairs, no problem.' Oh, God, I thought, bringing to mind a poster slapped up all over town: it showed an old Arab man bent double under the weight of a huge sack; inside the sack was the domed city of Jerusalem.

'Perhaps we shouldn't do this,' I said. 'I have a lot of heavy things, many books, weird things, sculptures.'

Ahmed looked hard at me, trying to figure out what kind of strange creature I might be. 'Let's go,' he said. I nodded agreement.

Ahmed laboured up and down stairs, his back piled high with boxes. When we hit the street to load up the car I would wince and hold my back in order to let passers-by know that I was incapacitated. Once, shamefully, I limped. As he worked, Ahmed told me about his good daughter at home in Beit Jallah, and his uncontrollable daughter in America. Her name was Yasmin and she had run away to New York with a boy from their village. Now she was working in a Manhattan hospital as a medical orderly. The boyfriend was sweeping floors. They wanted to be doctors. He seemed quite proud of his daughter's rebelliousness.

I told Ahmed about Rose. 'She's intelligent, she's beautiful, she's fun to be with, the joints of her thighs are like jewels (this last was a thought) and I'm going to marry her when she gets back.' Ahmed closed his eyes, as if to say, 'When they go, they don't return.'

After an hour I said, 'Okay, let's break. You look like you need a drink.'

'Ahmed replied, 'Ramadan,' and started to pick up more boxes. 'I'll drink at sunset,' he added. I sat down on an untaped carton of Rosie's clothes; the narrow strap of one of her nightdresses hung forlornly over the side. I looked at Ahmed. His thin face glistened, sweat had gathered in the creases of his forehead and was trickling in small rivulets down towards the matted reservoirs of his silver eyebrows.

'There is no choice,' he went on. 'I must work, and I must be observant.'

'You must stop,' I continued, trying to sound insistent. 'You can't fast when human life is threatened – it's in the Koran.' This was a wild grope, and we both knew it. Ahmed refused to pay me any attention. He heaved my drawing table up on to his back and wobbled towards the stairs.

Now I was caught. I wasn't new to guilt, it was one of the four food groups in my family, but this was a special pleasure. Idea for a movie: a scrawny old Arab guy who isn't permitted to eat or drink in the daytime hours has to move the belongings of a strong, well-fed, youngish Jewish sculptor from one part of Jerusalem to another. The YJS, while he is sympathetic to the old man's predicament, recognizes that he cannot tell him to stop because (1) the old man wants to work and needs the money and (2) it's not right to mess around with other people's gods. Later, the YJS's girlfriend returns from Tel Aviv; she is appalled by the whole episode; she leaves.

While I was trying to figure out how to proceed, the phone rang. I had sunk deep into Rosie's clothes and had to rock myself forward to get out of the box. Underwear and overwear tumbled to the floor. When I picked up the receiver I had a black dress strapped to my leg.

'Samuel?' Rosie's voice sounded very far away. 'I wanted to let you know I'm at Megged's.' Megged! I knew this guy. He worked with Rose, taking groups on trips into the Negev and showing them the flora and fauna. He was a handsome bastard. We had once spent an evening at his Little Tel Aviv apartment listening to an endless loop of birdsong tapes.

'What are you doing there?'

'We went out together to see sternbergia. Megged cried.'

'Sternberger?' I had known a Ronnie Sternberger at school. I'd heard that he had made a fortune in wastepaper baskets. But why was he in Israel? And how could he make Megged cry?

'Not Sternberger, you idiot,' Rose was saying, '*sternbergia*, the plant. We drove up to the Galilee. You should have been there.' (Yes, I thought, I should have.) 'There was an entire field. We had to go, it was our one chance before the rains come. Megged said it looked like a carpet of yellow. Is my father with you?'

'No,' I replied, 'Ahmed is.'

It was her turn to be mystified. 'Who's Ahmed?

'He's a friend.' (I could form attachments in her absence too.) 'By the way, we have a place, on Harakevet Street, number 23. It's a former gynaeceum. We're moving today.'

'That's great,' Rose said, but I could tell she'd already stopped listening, something was distracting her (probably the discrete cry of the redwing). 'Look after Dad,' she continued, 'he's lonely. I'll be back.'

I put the phone down. Ahmed was nowhere to be seen. I found him at the bottom of the stairs staring at a few pieces of broken skull that he had in his hands. He was panting heavily. 'It's okay,' I said, 'it's a bust I did in art school. It doesn't mean anything.'

We drove over to the new house and unloaded. I told Ahmed that I'd give him money for two full days if he stopped now and finished the rest tomorrow. I offered to pay him for the work he'd already done. He got insulted and gave me a short lecture on trust, honesty and faith. 'Okay,' I said, 'see you tomorrow.'

It was now late afternoon. The light over the railway tracks had taken on an ochre tinge that lent to the trees and dusky air an antique richness. I walked stiffly into my new home. Naomi had removed her trapeze, but the heavy circle hooks remained in the ceiling. With my foot I unrolled our double futon indented with two shapes that, somewhere around the middle, merged into one. I lay down gingerly on my back, on Rosie's side. I was in trouble, physically and emotionally, not big trouble to be sure, but trouble nevertheless. It is what we are born to, it springs out of the ground and jumps on our backs. We can't shake it.

I hated taking siestas, especially late ones, but I slept nevertheless. When I woke, my back had stiffened so completely that I had to roll off the futon in order to get out of bed. I crawled to the bathroom, ran water from a kneeling position, half stood, then lowered myself into the bath like an equipment-laden deep-sea diver tumbling backwards off a boat into the ocean. After soaking myself for an hour I was still in pain. There was a pharmacy downtown that stayed open late. I could have taken a bus, but I walked, hoping that the exercise and warm night air would combine to loosen me up.

In order to confound Rose and Megged, I walked through the prettiest streets I knew. I tried to pay close attention to the constituents of the natural world that were available to me on this cloudy, moonless night. You see, Rose and I had had this nature problem for a while. 'You love junk,' she had said to me back in the summer, during one of our evening rambles around town. 'You don't see flowers, only the junk that's crushing them.' She had knelt in a wild border, and tried to point out some flat yellow blooms. 'These are evening primroses, they open at sunset to attract the night insects.' But I had been taken by a megaphone-shaped piece of metal that someone had dumped on top of them. Rose got irate. 'You know who still cares about nature?' she said. 'Sunday painters. The rest of you, all you "serious artists", are holed up in factories decorating your "spaces" with junk.'

'We're making something beautiful out of the detritus of the late twentieth century,' I responded. 'And you know what, that cylinder could easily transform into a flower, it also has a shape, and colour. Moreover, on another level, we are what we discard. I'm holding a mirror up to garbage.' Rose snorted. The truth was I knew exactly what she was saying. I paid lip service to nature. For example, I loved the names of the specimens she brought home to classify – purple bugloss, star thistle, blue lotus – but I had long ago stopped looking at the flowers. Why? Too much Rauschenberg?

When I turned on to Balfour Street I lost track of these

art thoughts. A crowd had gathered, as usual, in front
of the Prime Minister's house. Men and women, mostly
young, huddled behind a police barrier. They held flash-
lights and lanterns and stood in silence under a large
sign, like a scoreboard, erected behind them. White letters
chalked on a black background announced the number of
the Lebanon war dead. Begin's house was floodlit, but
shuttered. He was said to be depressed. A great weight
had sunk from his brain down into his heart and anchored
there.

A voice called out to me from the crowd. It was Ada.
'Sam,' she said, 'your girlfriend was just here.'

'Rose?'

'Do you have other girlfriends?'

'That's impossible,' I said. 'I spoke to her a couple of
hours ago, she's in Tel Aviv.'

'Not any more.'

It was true that the drive from Tel Aviv to Jerusalem
took only forty minutes, so there was no reason why Rose
couldn't be back. If, that is, she had been in Tel Aviv in
the first place.

'Did she say where she was headed?' I asked, trying to
sound as if whatever answer Ada gave would concur with
knowledge I already had.

'No,' Ada replied (she was enjoying this). 'Don't you
know?'

I picked up my pills and got in a cab. Which home
should I go to? The one with the bed seemed more likely,
but maybe Rose was at the other. After all, she only had
a key to our old apartment. I went to Bezalel Street and
told the cabbie to wait. No Rose. I looked around the half-
empty apartment for a while as if she might materialize
out of the shadows, but if she was there she chose to
remain discarnate.

My driver, Natan Meshoulam, whose broad water-
buffalo shoulders took up half the front seat, fiddled with
the radio dial. When the news came on he listened care-

fully, then announced, 'We finish them good. No more Katyushas.' Then he found a music station he liked and, in a deep guttural voice, joined in with the song on the radio. 'Sleep sliding avay,' he sang, 'know ze nerrer to destination more you sleep sliding avay.'

In the early morning Morris and Ahmed showed up at the same time. I wanted to say, 'Hey, you both have uncontrollable daughters,' but I didn't. Even without my pressing on them what they had in common, they seemed to get on. Morris was particularly interested in the sheepskin vest that Ahmed was wearing. With Ahmed's permission he felt it, stuck his nose in the wool, and then, astonishingly, tried it on.

'Let me ask you something,' said Morris, pulling the material together at the front to cover his shirt and tie (I knew what was coming): 'What would a vest like this cost?'

'You tell me,' Ahmed replied. 'Guess.'

Oh, this was a delight, two cagey guys, neither giving an inch.

Morris named a price.

'Higher,' said Ahmed.

Morris tried again.

'Lower,' Ahmed responded. This might have gone on all morning if I hadn't intervened.

While Ahmed carried the rest of the heavy boxes downstairs, Morris moved the delicate pieces. I didn't even bother to hold my back. I had the oldest moving company in the world. I was beyond embarrassment.

'Let me tell you about fur,' said Morris as he and Ahmed packed the car. 'You know what happens on the streets of America? They spit. They spit at women in fur. Fur! That clothed us when we were naked. That kept us warm in the Ice Age. To wear fur is a human thing. It's in our nature.'

Soon, they moved on to skinning (Ahmed had witnessed his father do a few goats) and from there to tan-

ning. Daughters, I wanted to say, please talk about daughters. I need to understand. Or wives, at least wives. But
it was not to be. Morris said he would drive Ahmed back
to the Old City. I gave Morris money and asked him to
haggle over the final price. His eyes lit up. I told Ahmed
my girlfriend's father would be paying him. He looked at
me as if to say, 'Too cowardly to do your own bargaining,'
but I was in no mood for the thrust and counter-thrust of
financial debate. By lunchtime, I was alone in the house
by the railway tracks, standing rigid among my worldly
possessions, lonely as the pasha's daughters.

Four days later Rose came in through the door while I
was having breakfast. I was so happy and surprised that
I didn't even say, 'Where have you been?' Instead (the
sun streaming in with her, the fresh scents of morning
carried through on the breeze) I said, 'Want to walk?'

I thought I'd forgive her. I supposed she was allowed
her last-minute jitters. After all, I'd had them. However,
by the time we reached Abu Tor (we were heading for
the Old City) Rose had already put *me* on the spot. 'I can't
believe it,' she began. 'You've been going around town
asking everybody if you should marry me. Do you realize
how humiliating that is?'

I was nonplussed. 'How do you know that?' I asked,
which was a mistake – I should have gone for flat denial.

'First, your shrink has a mouth the size of the Grand
Canyon. Second, your friends can't be trusted. Third, this
city is a village. You know that. You wake up in the
morning and the neighbours know how you are before
you do.

'Okay,' I said, 'it was foolish of me. I admit it. But it
helped me to hear what I already knew. I'm in love with
you. I want to marry you.'

Rosie was silent. We passed the Cinematèque where an
Eric Rohmer Film Festival was playing. Then we crossed
the Sultan's Pool and headed uphill.

'There's something else,' she said. 'Megged. He understands something about me that you don't.'

I nearly said, 'Is this a pollination issue?' but I stopped myself. Megged. That flowery fuck. How did he get to be so deep and understanding? Of course, Rosie couldn't put into words what it was Megged had grasped about her. She had a feeling, that was all.

I had known for a long time that, where love is concerned, feelings can't be fought with reason, so I decided to beg and plead. By this time we had reached Jaffa gate. I was saying something that had no chance of being persuasive – 'Your father thinks we should live together for a year' – when I caught sight of Åhmed out of the corner of my eye. He was standing watching two men play backgammon. I called his name across the square. When he looked up I gestured towards Rosie, as if to say, 'See, she did come back.'

Ahmed looked right through me (Morris must have skinned him terribly in the bargaining), then he turned towards the wall where he had laid down his equipment and began to unwind his ropes. A sharp shaft of sunlight pierced Jaffa gate, like a diamond-cutter's knife, and cut me off from Rose.

Bank Holiday

We take the number 226 bus from Dollis Hill to Golders Green station. Along the way the houses expand and beautify. Then, we hop on the single-decker number 210 to Hampstead Heath. Dennis asks me, 'How many ears has Davy Crockett got?' I shake my head. 'Three,' he says. 'His left ear, his right ear, and his wild front ear.' As soon as we're off the bus we cross the no-man's-land near the Whitestone Pond, and enter the wild frontier of the Heath. No fooling around with the coconut shy, the penny roll, or even the bumper cars. We head straight for the Rat Woman. It is August 1967, and you can still catch a freak show at the fun fair.

At the entrance to the tent stands a throwback from the previous decade, a pointy-faced, vicious spiv, hair slicked back, Teddy Boy jacket, black drainpipe jeans, winkle-picker Chelsea boots covered in mud. He wants half a crown from each of us. Dennis says, 'Who are you – the Rat *Man*?' El spivo doesn't like this. He mentions something about slicing our fucking noses off. Dennis is extremely tough, so it's okay to laugh in his face and enter the tent.

It's very hot under the canvas and there's a pungent odour coming from the cage. At first we can't see her because there's a whole crowd of men (and a few women) standing in front of us trying to get a look. Okay, here she is, lying stretched out in this brown wire thing that looks as though it's been put together from old fire guards.

'What? Not even tits?' says an old geezer next to us, to no one in particular.

'Shut your *fucking* mouth,' the Rat Woman replies from her supine position.

She's in a full-body leotard: the top half is sheer, with tufts of brown hair glued over her nipples. The bottom is fake rat-skin with a long tail attached. She's got narrow, sharp-looking, protruding front teeth, which may have got her the job in the first place. It's not the tail that gets me, or the brown and white rats crawling all over her, as if she were in a sewer, it's her long, brown, varnished, witchy nails.

'Imagine being scratched by those,' I say to Dennis, nudging him and pointing.

'Nasty,' Dennis replies.

We're up close now with our faces almost pressed against the wire. I feel some bastard trying to pick my back pocket, but as there's nothing in it, he's going to be out of luck.

'Can I *do* something for you, gentlemen?' asks the Rat Woman, giving a heavy stare, and daring us to linger.

'Bite their balls off,' yells some loudmouth from the back of the crowd.

I say to the Rat Woman, 'Want some cheese?'

'I'll give you cheese,' she screams. 'I'll give you fucking cheese.'

Before I can get out of the way she scoops up a handful of rat shit and sawdust and throws it through the cage at my face. I try to duck but get caught behind the ear. I can feel little pellets in my hair.

We get down on our hands and knees and crawl to the side of the tent. Some kid is lying there trying to saw through one of the guy-ropes with a tiny penknife.

'What are you doing?' Dennis asks him, stupidly. He jabs the knife at us.

'Watch it,' I say (he's very small).

We roll out of the fetid tent into some muddy caravan ruts. Behind our heads the generator for the merry-go-round is giving off a high-pitched whine, as if it's going to explode.

'*Fun* fair. They call this a *fun* fair,' says Dennis.

'Well,' I reply, 'aren't you having fun?'

We scramble down the Heath to the lower part of the fair. Outside the Big Wheel, we bump into beautiful Pat McNally from our school, and her new boyfriend. 'This is Lemberg,' she says in her Wembley whine, 'he's an artist.' Dennis looks at me. I know what he's thinking. Pat's last boyfriend, Slim, was a consummate Mod: scooter, parka, big Who fan, the whole thing. But he's dead. Done in by the Chinese heroin that wafted into our school last year like a sweet summer breeze, then blew itself right up into a fat death wind. This guy, Lemberg, looks like a poor substitute for Slim. 'Wanna see his studio?' Pat asks us. She doesn't bother to tell him our names.

We stand in front of this huge canvas that is a portrait of naked Lemberg, giant-size, thick brushes in his hand, giant thick tube of a penis hanging down. A black scrawl in the bottom right-hand corner of the painting reads 'Drive your cart and your plough over the bones of the dead.'

Lemberg sits at the table in the middle of his studio rolling a joint. He's about thirty, maybe thirty-five.

'What's this, then?' says Dennis, pointing at the penis. 'You've been using your imagination a little, haven't you?'

'Oh no,' says Pat, matter-of-factly, 'he does have a big one. Don't you?'

Lemberg doesn't respond, he keeps sorting through his bag of grass. He's humming a little song to himself, like Winnie-the-Pooh: 'What you don't need/stalks and seeds'.

We respect almost anything Pat says (1) because of her recent bereavement, and (2) because she knows Twiggy. I have a third reason for respecting her. For some months she has been the object of all my fantasies, in most of which she is naked and hard at work.

Dennis starts to wander around the studio, picking up tubes of paint and squeezing blobs of colour onto his hands; then he wipes them on his jeans. 'Look,' he says, pointing at his trousers. 'Art.'

It seems all right to be thirty-five and an artist in trendy Hampstead. You get a big bed in the middle of an open space (it's rumpled, and a not-so-small patch of dry brown blood is on the under-sheet), this gorgeous sixteen-year-old girl who we're all, me especially, dying for, and you get to paint yourself naked. 'Leave the paint alone,' says Lemberg. Ah, he speaks. And what do you know? He's one of us. He's from our part of town. So there's not a lot we can do now, because he knows who we are, and we know who he is. That's all it takes in London really, someone opening their mouth.

We smoke the dope.

'This is home-grown,' says Lemberg.

'You should see his set-up,' Pat adds. 'There's a whole little room covered in tinfoil, with studio lights he got from a closed-down theatre.'

'Ever try hash-oil?' asks Lemberg. 'This is coated in hash-oil. Makes for a trippy experience.'

'What?' Dennis asks. 'Are you telling me we can expect to hallucinate?'

'What you expect, and what you get, may turn out to be two different things entirely.'

'Very meaningful,' Dennis replies.

After about ten minutes Dennis says to me 'It's big socks time.' He's referring to that moment when the dope-effects start to creep into your knees, then down towards your calves where they irritate the area just above where the sock-line would be if you were wearing big socks. Lemberg has moved over to Pat and is trying to kiss her. She keeps pushing his face away, but only in a kind of 'just-wait-till-they've-gone' way. We go.

Outside, I look at the normally invisible hairs on the back of my hand and see a waving cornfield. 'That's a hash-oil magnification you're experiencing,' says Dennis when I describe what's going on. 'Your powers of perception have been heightened.'

Soon after, I have this idea about running up an Israeli flag on our school flagpole. I use my sharpened powers to imagine a huge blue-and-white Star of David whipping in the wind over Brondesbury, and Queen's Park and Paddington. Last week Owen (Religious Instruction) beat me badly with the 'Kosher cosh' for talking in class. I have a deeper grudge against Beaglehole for humiliating me during gym. I was wearing red shorts instead of the regulation black. 'Wolfson,' he said, 'this isn't a Jewish fashion show.'

This kind of thing goes on all the time in our school ('Cohen, stand in the wastepaper bin, you're rubbish') which mingles semi-intelligent sociopaths from Kilburn with recidivist Jewish kids from Willesden and Wembley.

The question is: where to get the flag? Dennis, who has an agile but generally impractical mind, immediately suggests that we steal one. But from where? We stand outside a house with a blue plaque where John Keats lived two hundred years ago.

Dennis says, 'When was the last time you saw an Israeli flag? I mean one within graspable distance.'

I totter around on some blurry edge in my mind. I know where I'm going, but I don't quite want to get there. Eventually, I say, 'In synagogue, when your cousin Norman was bar mitzvah. Don't you remember? They unfurled it behind him when he got his trees.'

'What's the problem?' Dennis yells up in what he thinks is a whisper. I'm lying, like a fish on a platter, on one half of a huge hexagonal stained-glass window that we have managed to push open with a pole. I've scaled the concrete wall and the friable paint job is all over my hands and clothes. My face is up against the mane of a tawny Lion of Judah. The glass, bonded in metal, feels like it's going to shatter at any minute. Meanwhile, I'm tipping forward but can't slide through. I'm thinking about the fulcrum, and how poorly I did in Physics (26%; Highest in Form 97%; Diligence C; Comments: Lazy and incompetent') when suddenly I'm head first on the padded seats of the temple.

Someone has been here before us. The whole place is a mess. There are prayer books with pages torn out strewn all over the place and ripped prayer shawls on the floor. One of the red velvet curtains in front of the ark has been slashed, as have the puffy seats where the synagogue wardens sit in their shiny top hats and tails.

I let Dennis in through a side door. He looks around. 'Someone's been enjoying themselves,' he says. 'Any sign of the flag?'

Even I am appalled by his insouciance. 'This is a serious thing,' I say. We take a quick tour – it's mostly slashing and ripping. There is one piece of nasty artwork, a black swastika on one of the side walls, but it looks as if they ran out of paint. It occurs to us both, at about the same time, that if anyone were to come in now, we would have a lot of explaining to do.

We're on our way out (sans flag) when we hear the noise. It seems to be coming from the pipes in the organ loft. It's a tenebrous, adult-male groaning. When we get up there we find the janitor. His face is blotchy and bruised, there's a crescent of half-dried blood under each of his nostrils. 'I tried to stop 'em,' he says. 'Those bastards. They come in out of the park. What do they want to do a thing like this for?'

Dennis looks around; he's developing a little volcanic glow in his eyes. I've seen it before – it merges anger and impatience, and is sometimes a prelude to violence. 'Do you know where the flag is?' he asks.

'Who cares about the fucking flag?' I say, and for a moment it looks as if the two of us might get into a fight (not good for me).

For a while, the janitor and me try to clear up the mess. Dennis goes into the back office to look for the flag. I stuff a lot of the torn sheets into someone's box-seat. Then I get fed up, sit down and start reading. 'Lust not after her beauty in thine heart; neither let her take thee with her eyelids. For by means of a whorish woman a man is brought to a piece of bread.' What piece of bread? I try to think about Pat McNally's eyelids, but they're impossible to visualize. Eyebrows, yes, average thickness, blonde. A guide to her pubic hair? Could be.

The janitor says he's going to phone the police. Dennis appears with the flag (not quite as big as I'd hoped). He's already attached it to its staff. I ask the janitor, 'Mind if we borrow this for a while?' He shrugs, as if to say, 'Makes no difference now.'

Beyond the synagogue are the open fields of Gladstone Park. We unfurl the flag and run with it streaming behind us like a medieval banner. A couple of stray dogs chase us for a while; Dennis sends them off by aiming kicks towards their faces. Kids are on the swings, and forming queues up by the stone fountain. In the distance, past the muddy duck pond, a rainbow arches over the weeping willows and high, thin branches of the silver birches. It must have rained while we were inside. A small girl comes up to us. She says, 'I know how doggies talk.' She gives a few yelps, then a growl, followed by a heavy bark.

Outside Electric House on Willesden Lane we wait a long time for a bus. Then they don't want to let us on with the flag. There's an inspector on board. 'Suppose we stop suddenly,' he says. 'You could lance that right through someone's lungs.'

The conductor adds, 'More like driving a stake through a person's heart.'

Dennis says, 'Or sticking a javelin up your arse.' We walk.

On the way I try to get Dennis to talk about something that matters. What I want to get at is this: why would an attractive sixteen-year-old girl give herself over, body and possibly soul, to someone like Lemberg? Now, from Lemberg's point of view it's all very clear – he wants to crush her bones. But from Pat's?

Of course, I have this special interest. In the immediate post-Slim mourning period ('Drive your cart and your plough over the bones of the dead') I had one slow dance with Pat at the Starlite Ballroom, Greenford. She wore a black mini-skirt, with a semi-transparent pink blouse that revealed something she told me was called a 'no-bra bra'. On the one hand she seemed impalpable as pink steam, on the other hand, her body's imprint, as if I were sand, lasted all night.

When I broach the subject with Dennis I quickly discover that he has no interest in the whys and wherefores of anything. He is all business and to the point. The solid rope of dailiness is what he likes to climb. If I were to say now, as I feel like saying, 'I'm losing my enthusiasm for this flag adventure because the day has already thrown up more than I can digest,' he would turn on me.

Once, Dennis brought an axe to school. During lunchbreak he chopped up his desk. At first, I thought this was a familiar, if extreme, assault upon the seat of learning. Then I realized he was trying to break the frozen sea within him. We stuffed the splintered wood in our gym bags, took the afternoon off, and threw it, piece by piece, onto the platforms of deserted stations: Queensbury and Canons Park, the northern end of the old Bakerloo line.

But is this what I really want? Vandalism and adventure? All summer I have been carrying around the possibilities for change, for shifting my allegiances. They rise and fall, like unexpected adolescent erections, and, appropriately, converge on issues of hardness and softness. I am awed by the former, embodied in Dennis, but generally inclined, by temperament and character, toward the latter. Somewhere inside I want to surround a girl, well,

Pat McNally, with the most insipid and conventional accoutrements of love.

Now, don't get me wrong, I had seen the brown-red stain on Lemberg's bed, and I knew all about the body's betrayals. What is more, almost my entire education in the sex area derived from dirty jokes, poorly photographed barber's shop magazines, and badly drawn graffiti. The previous year, in order to counterbalance my developing vulgarity, my father had dragged me, one Friday night, to a small Sephardic synagogue in London's East End. He wanted me to hear a group of old men chant the Song of Songs, or Canticle of Canticles as it was called in the prayer book (I read this, of course, as 'Testicle of Testicles'). But even though I had listened and learned about the little foxes, the breasts like young roes feeding among the lilies, and the importance of eating the honeycomb with the honey, the notion of a higher love had not really penetrated. It is not until now, walking down Salisbury Road with this stupid flag, that the weak sun of consideration and love, hidden all season long, begins to penetrate the thick clouds of boorishness and lust that are gathered around me.

What I want, I now realize, is more Pat Woman than Rat Woman. Lemberg's bed has been a reminder that you can't have one without the other, but I have reached a decision to approach the hybrid with poetry, rather than teenage aggression. I begin this excursion into 'softness' by saying to Dennis, 'Do you know whose house we were outside back in Hampstead?'

'No.'

'Keats's.'

'So fucking what?'

This is no more than I expect, but the fact that I have raised the subject is, in itself, a significant beginning.

We arrive at the school. It is late afternoon. The turbulent sun is sending a bright glare to heat things up. Dennis has red hair, and because, at this moment, it matches the colour of the sun, I start to feel oppressed by Dennis's head. I say, 'Why don't you go and raise the flag yourself?'

'What?' he replies. 'After coming all this way?'

He tries to fire me up by repeating some heinous teacher acts. 'Do you remember when Fanny wouldn't let Sless go home early on Friday nights? How about when Fogwell threw you against the wall after your father wrote that bar-mitzvah-lesson note?' But this is second-division stuff, and Dennis knows it. He hadn't cared himself that Sless walked five miles to his Orthodox home instead of catching the bus. He had laughed, along with all the others, when I had my encounter with the wall.

'No,' I say. 'You go up there. I've had it.' Dennis starts to move very fast. For a moment I feel as if I'm a part of observed Nature. Off-screen, someone is whispering, 'The alpha male, by displaying resolution, and a sense of urgency, wishes to indicate that his companion is a coward.' Dennis throws the flag over the fence and climbs after it. I figure he'll have to get up on the gym roof, which may take him a while, and then make his way along to the crenellated turret that houses the flagpole. I've got at least twenty minutes.

I head into Queen's Park, and start walking towards the bandstand. I think I'll find some shade, stretch out, meditate. Considering it's a holiday the place is oddly deserted. Then I see why. About twenty teenagers are standing near the Pitch and Putt. They're carrying bicycle chains, golf clubs that they have stolen out of the shed, and some long sticks. They're on me before I can even think about running. I recognize a couple of psychopaths from the school a hundred yards down the road from our own.

First, it seems, they want to play. One of them, *homo Kilburnus stupidens*, says, 'I didn't know Jews were allowed in this park.'

His chief mate, a boy with a deceivingly innocent outbreak of summer freckles on his face, and a peacock tattooed on his bare chest, affirms, 'They're not.'

'So what are you doing here? Because you are a Jew. You are a *fucking* Jew, aren't you?'

I say, 'Yes.' This isn't bravery or defiance, because it absolutely doesn't matter what I say – 'A Thing of Beauty is a Joy Forever' or 'Fuck You, I'm Episcopalian', the consequences are going to be the same.

In case you think I'm taking all this with an air of cool detachment, I'm not. I shake and sweat and wait to get hit. There's a short interval while Freckles chivalrously challenges me to fight. I say, 'No thanks.' Then he belts me in the face with a set of brass knuckles. I make myself fall down, and cover my head with my hands. I can feel the kicks coming in: nasty, sharp ones in the kidneys, and one to the head that feels as if it's broken my fingers. I'm praying that they lay off with the driving irons. I cry, choke, and bleed. For a moment I think they've stopped. I cough, and each breath brings a dragging, boiling, bubbling sound. But they're not done. Two of them pull out my arms while a third presses something into my back. A knife! I scream. They laugh. The bastards are all laughing. Someone says, 'Fuck off out of here.' I run, dribbling blood and mucus from my nose. Obviously, I haven't been stabbed. I feel on my back: nothing. I reach a water fountain, sip, spit, and sip again. It is only when I take off my T-shirt to wipe my face that I see what they've done. Where once there was a blank, white space, the word JOO is now inscribed; two 'O's – jocularity or ignorance? I pull the stained, soaking T-shirt back on. It's hot enough to walk bare-chested, but I've been exposed, and I want to cover myself.

In the shade of a grey slate roof my bodyguard is asleep. The Israeli flag, that I had imagined rippling in waves of triumph, shiny point of resistance in a constellation of hostility, droops in the windless early dusk. I can't blame Dennis for what has happened to me, although I sort of want to. We are thrown unprotected on the free, spinning world, and you have to take the blows when they come. They do come.

I try to think my beating through, and on the way to the bus stop I half manage it. I feel angry and impotent, no doubt about that. For a while though, I advance a wounded soldier aspect to what I have been through. I say to myself: This is not all that unpleasant, it's like the bruised fatigue that follows a hard soccer game. Then my kidneys start to ache, and I touch my swollen lips. Suddenly, I find myself in tears. There is nothing redeeming about my pain. It is hurt and humiliation, pure and simple, with its own vectors and swoops.

By the time I get back to Lemberg's, which takes a while because I have trouble remembering where he lives, it's dark. There are iron clouds stamped in a blue-black sky and all the warmth of the day has gone down with the sun. When she opens the door Pat looks at me, fails to register any shock, and says, 'Been fightin'?' Over her shoulder I see Lemberg at work. He's directing a nude model, a skinny girl with long black hair and conical breasts like salt-shakers. I suppose he's going to sketch her. As I move in through the door the girl takes up a pose, Lemberg moves close and adjusts her limbs.

Pat leads me past the artist at work. There's a bright, naked light bulb hanging over the table in the kitchen area. I want to be in darkness. I must communicate this in some way, because after I have washed the caked blood from my face, and reviewed the copper bruises on my jaw and around my cheekbones, Pat says, 'Wanna go to the pictures?'

In the Hampstead Everyman I think, for about an hour and a half, that I might take hold of her hand, but in the end I don't.

Savyon

The streets of Savyon, a suburb east of Tel Aviv, are Israel's only Millionaire's Rows. To go there is to enter a fabulous world: the houses are oversized, the cars too shiny. The town is out of place in Israel: when you drive through it looks as if it might have blown in that morning on a hot desert wind from California.

I was in Savyon with someone else's boyfriend (money goes together with all kinds of wickedness) when the Doron boy was kidnapped. The police patrols were stepped up and the electric gates of the expensive homes hummed shut. An ancient crime had finally been delivered to Modern Israel. 'You know what this means, Liora?' Ephraim asked me. 'It means we're not all one big family after all. A family that fights, but in which, essentially, each member has the other's best interests at heart. No more carpet slippers.' I knew what he meant. On the streets I had often seen people walking in rubber-soled slippers, symbols of domestic ease in the public place.

I hadn't planned to stay long (a two-, maybe three-night stand) but then the police announced that they wanted to interview everyone in the immediate neighbourhood. They even set up a road-block. So I was stuck. Ephraim's girlfriend, the real girlfriend, was due down for the week-end. In order to make everything look normal Ephraim said he would invite a male friend of his over. 'You'll like him,' he said. 'He's a journalist, he edits the literary supplement of one of the big newspapers. He's just another lonely soul.'

'That doesn't make us a match,' I replied. I always

resented it when people mistook my single status and sexual enthusiasm for desperation.

Ephraim planned to tell Tamar that he was playing matchmaker, introducing two old friends, setting them up. I said 'Okay, but no creeping up on me in the shower, and stuff like that.'

I wasn't pleased with myself. I believe, deep down, that women really are a sisterhood. But there is also desire, and sometimes, especially after you have been bumming around in the desert for a few months, as I had, there is an overwhelming desire for comfort. I had bumped into a rich guy, offering cooked food (prepared by hired staff), hot showers, a comfortable bed. I am not alone in my weakness for the consolations of luxury. Even Gloria Steinem, I read recently, when she was feeling vulnerable, gave herself over for a while to a millionaire developer/industrialist. He offered a limo-cocoon, and she crept in.

The house wasn't Ephraim's. It belonged to his grandfather Shimon Tapoz, who had made a fortune in tinned fish, tuna mainly, and owned factories all over continental Europe. Not only a stellar businessman, Shimon was also an ardent Zionist, and religious to boot. So, one day after the Six Day War, he scrubbed the fish smell off his clothes, moved his profits from Belgium to Israel, and built his dream house on what was then a sandy space in the hinterland of the big city.

All this I picked up, along with Ephraim, on the first night we spent together under the desert stars. It was a hot, passionate few hours, although making love in the sand does have its uncomfortable aspects. I had been living on Coral Beach, near Eilat, for three months, selling cotton T-shirts from the aquarium that I'd been attached to, and smoking a little, well a lot of, marijuana. I wasn't unhappy but I was starting to get somewhat unhinged. I sat around most of the day under clear blue skies trying to figure out whether I was a good or a hurtful person. My last relationship, with the head of my research programme, had ended badly. He had caught me with another man, *in flagrante delicto*. I should never have given him the key.

Also, walking around all day on a nude beach taking in varieties of genitalia – so much *hanging* – was slowly eroding my sex drive. So when this fully clothed, rather good-looking guy *drove* onto the beach in his little *deux chevaux*, annoying everybody and begging for some attention, I gave it to him. The ostentatious type isn't usually mine but, on the other hand, I thrive on unpredictability and, in any case, Ephraim didn't seem like too much of a jerk.

The police in Savyon wanted to interview the staff first. If the case hadn't been so horrible I think I might have been more excited. Ephraim actually had to call someone in from the garden to be questioned. But I had seen the child's picture in the paper, and all intriguing *policier* aspects were subdued by my sympathetic anxieties. Like most other people, certain childhood separations, evenings with nasty baby-sitters or scary relatives, had disposed my imagination to events like these. I still recalled vividly getting lost at the age of five on a Cape Cod beach and the kind gentleman (was he kind?) who helped me find my parents.

The collective first thought, of course, was 'Arabs'. But the phone calls to the family put paid to that theory. The local accent was too strong; the enemy was unmistakably within. Even so, before approaching *us* the two detectives covering Ephraim's street (cute young guys in plain clothes) wanted the Filipino cook to interrupt her vegetable dicing, and the Palestinian gardener temporarily to cease his tree-pruning, in order to explain where they had been last Monday morning, who they had seen, and what, if anything, they knew that might help the police in their inquiries. When they were done, they told Ephraim they would return the next day to interview 'you and your wife'. 'She's just a friend,' Ephraim replied hastily, as if he were already explaining my presence to Tamar.

We had one night to kill before she showed up, and we spent it in the master bedroom. Before bed, we played around for a while in the sunken tub with built-in jacuzzi. The whole thing was all very Hollywood; lavishness and indulgence are odd for Israel. I was warming to Ephraim beyond his chiselled good looks and hard body. He seemed to be a person who thought about things. He was in the family business 'learning the ropes', but I couldn't really hold this against him, or the fact that one day he would inherit millions. He had, too, a nice sense of the absurd. His big plan was to establish his own line of imports for orthodox Jews. There was a fish in Japan, he told me, that looked and tasted almost exactly like shrimp, but wasn't a shellfish. In other words it was kosher. Ephraim wanted to corner the market, import, can and sell under the brand name/slogan 'Zeh Loh Shrimp!'; translation: 'It's not Shrimp!'

In the morning, before the detectives returned, I went out by myself to swim laps in the pool. I ate breakfast on a patio overhung with climbing rose bushes not yet in bloom and surrounded by delicately scented shrubs. All around me were the noises that accompany the rich at leisure: the scrape and mow of gardening crews, the hypnotic ticking of multiple sprinklers, the secure, dull thunk of ball on racquet. Beyond a nearby wall the neighbour's children dived and splashed in their own private pool. Were they scared? They didn't sound it. Nevertheless, I thought to myself: it's been exposed, the hush-hush life of the Savyon rich.

The handsome detectives arrived in the late morning. There wasn't much that I could tell them. I had drifted in out of the desert with the grandson of the manse. I knew about the kidnapping from the *Jerusalem Post*. Halfway into the conversation, however, I started to feel, from the intense way that they questioned me, that I was being stamped with the profile of the classic psycho-loner. No, I had no relatives in Israel. No, no actual job at the moment, although I had been working the previous year at the Underwater Observatory, and if they wanted references . . . No, I wasn't married. I didn't have children (but I certainly didn't mean them any harm). I was thirty. Yes, it was true that although I had blond hair and grey eyes I was Jewish. (When I walked down the streets of an Israeli city men called out to me: 'Germany?', 'Sweden?') At the end of our dialogue, the one who I had decided wasn't so handsome after all asked me how much longer I planned to be in Israel and if I'd like to accompany him on a brief tour of the often-overlooked-by-tourists beautiful reaches of the Upper Galilee.

Ephraim's interrogation lasted a lot longer than mine. Not surprisingly – he was a near neighbour and he knew the Doron family. He had been on cordial terms with the father, a brash, aggressive man who had made his money in the construction business and become something of a public figure because he was the contractor responsible for a great deal of new housing on the West Bank. But whatever he thought of Mr Doron as a person, Ephraim wouldn't have wished his child kidnapped. As everybody in the country now knew, a million-dollar ransom had been demanded. A hundred yards away a ring of police circled the Doron house. The parents had been given forty-eight hours to come up with the money.

After the police left, I walked to the end of the street and stood at the barrier that had been erected to prevent further passage. It was mid-morning, the sun was high and bright, trying its best to penetrate the cool, indifferent dwellings of the rich. There was quite a crowd at the metal gates: TV and radio crews, people with binoculars, a group of Arab cleaning women in headscarves and brightly coloured cotton dresses, their buckets and scrubbing brushes set aside as they awaited permission from the police to pass through to their domestic jobs.

Beyond the barrier, some fifty yards distant, was the Doron house: a towering, red-tiled edifice, built in the Provençal style. In the front, behind a low wall, a line of Judas trees had been planted. The saplings were all in bloom, their butterfly-shaped dark purple flowers dressing the trees from head to foot. The boy had been snatched from under these trees while riding his bicycle. Now, in the negligible shade thrown by the thin purple branches, four or five women stood weeping; I could hear them from where I stood. They must have been relatives, or close friends, for they soon made their way up the long driveway towards the house, and disappeared out of sight. I stared at the spray-painted yellow circle that marked where Avi Doron's bicycle had clattered to the ground. My stomach turned. What was it to be grabbed out of your life into terror?

Suddenly, I started to feel guilty for the night before, not only because of Ephraim's betrayal (my betrayal?), but also because I had had so much fun in proximity to so much pain. Why was I tormenting myself? I knew it was stupid but somehow the shame wouldn't go away.

Eventually, I had to recognize that this was simply another manifestation of the strange state that I had been in for some time. One night a few weeks previously I had left my Coral Beach lodgings (a sleeping bag) and taken a trip into Eilat. I sat in a run-down cinema with a bunch of rowdy locals and watched Woody Allen's *Crimes and Misdemeanours*. The audience crunched and spat sunflower seeds. Then, they rolled Coke bottles down the aisles. They were bored. And why shouldn't they be? The tip of the desert is no place for nuanced Manhattan behaviour. I, on the other hand, was riveted, and not only because I was smashed. Woody, it seemed to me, was asking the same questions that had clogged my head like a dust-storm during my weeks of desert somnambulism.

What was a crime? What was a misdemeanour? And

what was nothing at all? Everybody I knew seemed certain of the distinctions. This was rarely the case with me, especially where sex was concerned. I believed that in regard to sex, the garish deviation of rape excepted, it was almost impossible to discriminate. Misdemeanours simply were the way of all flesh, and therefore they were nothing at all. For that reason, I had never got exercised about infidelity, either for me or against me. I realized, of course, that such neutrality was bound to get me into trouble, and it did. Worse, I had never understood why I exhibited such a strange moral peculiarity: was it my normal-as-the-next-person's upbringing? Something I'd read at an impressionable age? Perhaps my weirdness about relationships explains what drew me to marine biology in the first place. I could have gone into one of the talkier disciplines, sociology or psychology. I'd excelled in them both at college. But studying plant life on the seabed didn't involve contemplating who owes what to whom in a relationship; taxonomy could be an end in itself.

Someone nudged me in the ribs. It was a small woman holding an armful of groceries tight to her chest. 'What do you think?' she asked. 'Is he dead? Is the boy dead?' I turned and walked back to the Tapoz house. I thought I'd try to talk to the police. Surely they'd let me go.

But Tamar had already shown up, and as soon as I walked in the door Ephraim was busy with fake, effusive introductions. Tamar was small and thin, with the short page-boy haircut so favoured by Israeli women, and a clear, honest face. I think she knew immediately that I'd been sleeping with her boyfriend, it was all there in the handshake. But, when it's convenient, and where betrayal is concerned it is often convenient, most of us can put aside what we instinctively know for fairly long periods of time.

Irene called out from the kitchen that lunch was ready. We took our places around the table and began an inevitably morbid conversation. Tamar was devastated by the kidnapping. Israel had lost its soul. What had happened was a symbol of the general decline in community values, yet another indicator, like the rise in materialism, that the country was doomed to become 'just like America'. Ephraim tried to console her: 'It's the work of one crazy individual,' he said. 'The event has no representative value.' I knew that he didn't believe this. I looked across at Tamar. She had hardly touched her food and her eyes were flicking back and forth from Ephraim to me, trying to figure out the precise connection between us.

We moved into the spacious lounge and watched TV for a while. The parents were waiting to hear again from the kidnapper. They had received a video tape, not released to the press. It was believed to show the boy alive and talking. Would the ransom be paid? Abruptly the studio discussion was interrupted. Mrs Doron, taking deep breaths and fighting back tears, came on screen to plead with the kidnapper not to hurt her son. Her husband stood behind her. When it was his turn to speak he announced what he called 'a sealed number' at which he could be contacted. He gave firm assurances that despite the police presence at his house they would not be allowed to moniter the ransom arrangements. He would follow all instructions.

It was a beautiful spring day, a beckoning light came in through the long French windows, crossed the shiny grand piano and obscured the faces on the TV screen. Ephraim suggested that Tamar and I play tennis. This seemed such a hopeless (and cruel) fantasy of his enjoying us in competition that I immediately said no. But Tamar asked 'Why not?' and insisted that I follow her out to the dusty red court. She proceeded to smash the ball at me with unrelenting ferocity. She probably wouldn't have admitted it, but she really did want to hurt me. The thing was, I couldn't blame her. I knew exactly what I had done, even if she didn't. By the end of our game, feeling sweaty and disgusted with myself, I went off to shower.

Standing under the streaming water I began to feel, in addition to everything else, disappointed. Why? Because Ephraim, scrupulously following my instructions, had failed to burst in on me. Here, I thought to myself, is your problem.

When I came out of the bathroom I walked past the guest bedroom. Through a half-open door, I saw a man (my phoney date, presumably) whispering like crazy into the telephone. I stopped for a moment, long enough to see him put the phone down, rush to the window, then run back to the phone and begin whispering again. He looked up and noticed me watching him. He put his hand over the receiver and said, 'It's my paper. Thought I'd give them a little atmosphere, seeing as I'm on the spot.' I moved on down the corridor.

I hadn't intended to keep on creeping about but it seemed that everywhere I went a private conversation was in progress. I had dressed and gone down to the kitchen to see if the cook needed help (it was strange how quickly the pleasures of being served wore off). Ephraim and Tamar were drinking tea at the table and didn't hear me approaching. I heard Ephraim say, very sweetly and innocently, 'Do you think they'll hit it off?'

Tamar replied, 'How exactly do you know her?' Suddenly, I was reeling. I felt, simultaneously, jealousy and joy. I wanted Ephraim exclusively, and this was not a feeling I was familiar with. On the other hand, as part-time lover I was free from the disturbances of a relationship in which the boyfriend was a cheat. Mix in doses of self-loathing and hatred of Ephraim and you have some idea of what I had concocted.

By dinner I felt really lousy. Tamar leaned on Ephraim's arm throughout the meal, laying a claim, while Ephraim's friend, Yuval, began to act as if I belonged to him by a kind of *droit du seigneur*. What was making things different for me this time? The big world outside was contorting the little world inside in ugly and confusing ways.

Tamar kept saying, 'That poor child. Suppose he never sees his parents again.' The more she talked about the kidnapping, the more ashamed of myself I felt about the affair. Was this a moral failure on my part? Terrible narcissism?

Ephraim, who could now barely look at me, kept shaking his head from side to side and repeating, 'Who would do a thing like that?'

The bouquet of spring flowers in the middle of the table, freshly cut from the family garden, started to take on a funereal quality. Yuval wanted to know what on earth I was doing in Israel. I told him laconically: 'I'm a marine biologist, I came from the Woods Hole Oceanographic Institute a year ago to do some work identifying specimens in the Gulf of Aqaba. My sabbatical ended but I stayed. I liked the desert and the Red Sea. I didn't want to go back to Massachusetts.'

The floodlights that ringed the house came on. The long, rectangular pool lit up uncannily blue; a tiny grove of orange trees miraculously assumed a celestial aura. A chorus of dogs, guard dogs presumably, sent up whines and barks from all the neighbouring gardens. Our conversation was receiving all the protection possible.

Yuval got up and left the room to make another phone call. He came back in a hurry. 'They caught him,' he said excitedly. 'He ran the father all over North Tel Aviv, then up to the bridge over the Yarkon. He used a flashlight, had him drop the money into a culvert. The police went after him.'

'But what about the boy?' Tamar broke in. 'Did they find the child?'

Yuval continued as if he hadn't heard her: 'Turns out he was an employee with a grudge. They caught up with him halfway to Netanya—'

'But the boy?' Tamar was insistent.

Yuval stopped. 'He won't say where he's hidden him.'

'They'll make him,' Ephraim said authoritatively. 'It won't take long.'

We moved out to the front of the house. The street was lit up like a movie set. A helicopter, its red tail-lights blinking, circled over the Doron house. A policewoman on a horse turned in caracoles before the crowd pressing up to the barrier. Camera crews scuttled everywhere, reporters argued with police, begging for access to the family. 'What a circus,' I said to Yuval. 'Don't you want to call this in?'

I thought I was being cutting, but he replied softly, 'No, no need.'

I decided to go to bed early. I would be able to leave in the morning, and there was nothing to keep me here now. I lay down on the double bed in the new room that I had been allocated by Ephraim (before moving we had checked carefully for loose clothes left in the master bedroom). I should probably have stayed in the desert. The water was warm and translucent. I had spent hours watching the colours change from red to purple-brown on the hills across the Gulf, in Jordan. True, I'd been alone and perplexed, but so what? It was better than this. Desire had led me to a street of misery. I turned my face into the pillow.

I would have cried for a long time, but Yuval pushed the door open and came in. 'Hey,' I said, as he approached the bed, 'before you get any ideas, I'm feeling *very* irritable, my whole body aches from tennis, and if you come any further into this room I may kill you.'

I shouldn't have said the words 'my whole body', they only excited him. 'How about a massage? To relieve the tension?'

'Please,' I said. 'Go away.'

'I know what's been going on,' Yuval continued. 'Ephraim is my oldest friend. I wasn't invited here to meet you but to protect him. I was happy to do it, but I'm attracted to you. Come on, I could blow the whole thing open if I wanted to.'

Was this sleaze-bag blackmailing me? 'It's not me you'd hurt,' I replied. 'I'm getting out of here. And just for future reference that's a very poor kind of come-on. Isn't it time for you to make a phone call?'

'She's probably asleep. She goes to bed early.'

'Who?'

'My wife.'

Oh! I had fallen among thieves! Dirt-bags, low-lifes, the cream of the scum. I had been set up and set down. What was it school teachers always said of cheats? 'Life will cheat them.' 'When you cheat you only cheat yourself.'

'Your wife! Your fucking wife. I thought you worked for the papers.'

'I do. I'm a literary editor.'

He lunged towards me. He seemed quite serious about his intentions so I was obliged to roll to the other side of the bed, get up quickly, and threaten him again. 'Don't you lay a fucking *finger* on me,' I said.

He started muttering something about American women. I don't know how things might have progressed, but our nocturnal struggle was interrupted by the pitch and whine of sirens under the window. We heard Ephraim running to the front door, and then Tamar scuttling up the stairs. She called out for Yuval. When he didn't respond she came into my room. A look of disgust crossed her face when she saw us, but I wasn't going to give her the satisfaction of an explanation. The siren from one car deviated into an endless wail, a yellow spotlight moved across the bedroom windows. Ephraim yelled up for us all to come down.

We walked beyond the tennis court and the swimming pool, past the aromatic orange grove and the thin line of lemon trees, to the farthest corner of the Tapoz's two acres. We stopped near a rank-smelling compost heap where bags of fertilizer and lime had been stacked next to two young saplings ready for planting. He was small, with a fleshy nose and large, dark eyes. His face was red and puffy from the beating he had received and there was blood caked in one of his ears. Every so often he would try to raise one of his handcuffed hands to swat at a mosquito, but the policemen would force it down again. As he turned to show them where to dig, his body, in the stark white light thrown by the spotlights, seemed to lose substance: in profile he looked as if he might have been cut from a piece of tin. Ephraim and Tamar clung to each other, Yuval hovered behind them. When the police began to shovel I moved round to the other side of the circle. After about half an hour, they pulled the body up out of the ground. I don't know why I thought I had to look, but I did. The corpse was ivory, the hair matted, the neck twisted and bruised, the head rested limply on a policeman's shoulder.

I went inside and packed my bag. Yuval followed. I declined his offer of a lift and walked out of the house and down to the bus stop. There was a police car sitting at the end of the street, a revolving blue light on its roof. As I passed, the driver leaned a little out his window. 'Where are you from?' he asked. 'Holland?'

Migrants

In hot, dusty June, Joel and Nancy Braverman sat in their small, clean kitchen in the East Talpiot Absorption Centre. The children were outside with a group. It was the first time that they had been alone since the move. Through the open window a babble of tongues filtered up to them, the loudest coming from the Russians in the apartment beneath. They looked at each other and laughed. Their situation was so absurd, the change in their lives so great, that a comic acceptance of the fate Joel had designed seemed, at this moment anyway, the only possible response.

How had they got here? It had begun like this. Joel, driving home on grey, rainy Route 128, heard the first missiles fall on Tel Aviv. The radio whistled and shrieked, sirens whined. Ten thousand miles away a relief vehicle sputtered to life. Then, a bang, a thump; what might have been Joel's briefcase jolting from the back seat onto the floor of his car turned out to be the Middle East correspondent adjusting his equipment. Everything went dead. Rain, sweeping in sheets over the reservoir that flanked the right-hand side of the highway, doused Joel's windshield faster than the wipers of his old Honda could handle. Silence from the radio, dead air, the slick beat of windshield wipers, and then, mercifully, Joel, along with millions of other listeners, was returned to the studio in Washington.

Although he had only visited Israel twice, once as a teenager, summer-working on a kibbutz, and once on his honeymoon, Joel felt powerfully drawn in. Stuck in traffic, stuttering forward, watching, without thinking, for the brake-lights on the truck in front to vanish then reappear, Joel focussed all his attention on the voice from the radio. The connection was restored. He was back in the Middle East. Were those screams he was hearing? The correspondent was panting, talking while running. Back in Washington they were telling him not to be silly, to put his gas-mask on. To hell with the listeners back home.

Joel turned off the highway, listening intently to an army spokesman recount the damage done by an Iraqi Scud to an outlying suburb of Tel Aviv. As he drove down the familiar, tree-lined streets, Joel began to feel as if his own quiet suburb, his house with its backyard basketball net and swing-set, his own children, were under attack. When he came into the house, Nancy had the TV on. The screen would go dark, then streak with light. Panic seeped into his living room. 'I can't bear it,' said Nancy.

The next morning, on his way to buy milk, Joel had the revelation. Everyone on the street was going about their business as if nothing had happened. 'I shouldn't be here,' he thought, surprised at himself, 'I should be there.'

Over breakfast, before Joel could finish explaining what he was feeling to Nancy, she interrupted him. 'What about schools?' she wanted to know. She also wanted to know about the language barrier, the army, Joel's job – he had been at Digital for fifteen years, he was high-up, highly paid. And what about *her* job? Her patients? How could she abandon them? How could she be a social-psychologist in Israel? All in all, had Joel really thought any of this through?

'I'm just talking about a feeling,' said Joel, 'not a decision.'

But, although he could not admit it to Nancy, he felt curiously resolved, as if a very powerful, and unacknowledged, part of his being had begun to work solidly, and irresistibly, against his own common sense. Over coffee, watching the morning news on CNN, Joel saw the tracer bullets over Baghdad as small, illuminated hyphens speedily separating his Jewish from his American self.

Weeks passed, Joel's commitment hardened. He saw that Nancy was tired of him, exhausted by his growing depression, but he couldn't seem to do anything about it. He was miserable when he came home from work. At night he turned on the TV, then, almost immediately, went to sleep. Would he ever wake up? He told her he was living a life that he didn't inhabit. She replied that she felt manipulated. He wanted to cut her off at the roots, to put their children in danger.

He went to the library and brought home an armful of books on Israel. He intended for her to read them (*his* mind was already made up) but they lay unopened on the chair in the front hall where he had dropped them. And then, out of the blue, she lost her job. Health services in Massachusetts were on the rocks, but they had always thought that Nancy's clinic was secure. Nancy began looking for work, but there were thousands of people like her on the job market. Joel, relentless, set off an insistent beat in her head. It said: 'Change your life.'

Late in spring she began to yield. Joel saw it first in the questions she began to ask: What was the winter like in Jerusalem? What was the exact length of army service? Could Zach come back for college if he wanted to? She attended a reading by a visiting Israeli poet. He overheard her on the phone telling a friend that she was 'sick of the "burbs", sick of what Reagan and Bush had done to the country. The rich had lost their sense of shame. It was all so boring.

The Bravermans discussed their 'still very tentative' plans with their best friends, Randy and Sara Shafer. The Shafers were shocked. Zionism was a word that had disappeared from their vocabulary. Israel, for them, if not altogether *discredited*, was certainly *tainted*, an embarrassment.

'What are you going to do, Joel? Bop Palestinians over the head?' asked Randy.

'They've got enough trouble finding jobs and homes for the Russians,' Sara added. 'What can Americans do there?'

And then came the inevitable question: 'What do you have in mind for the kids?'

Ah, the kids. The younger one wasn't such a problem. He was bewildered, but he would follow his Mommy and Daddy anywhere without a fight. But fifteen-year-old Zachary was adamant. He wasn't going any place where there wasn't major league baseball.

Joel and Nancy began to withdraw from the life around them. Against advice (the market was low) they sold the house, and the cars. What they did not ship in the way of furniture (the Shafers had given them matching yellow director's chairs with their names printed on the backs) they stored on the third floor of Nancy's parents' place. And then, as soon as school was out for the year, they were ready to leave.

In the El Al plane, rising through dark storm clouds over Boston, Nancy asked, 'Is this a big mistake?'

Joel, busy sounding out in English phonetics *One Hundred Hebrew Words*, looked up from his airline pamphlet. 'The word for "bird,"' he replied over the muffled roar of the jet's engines, 'seems to be the same as the word for "story".'

The Bravermans were surrounded by Russians. On the stairways and in the elevators they heard more Russian than Hebrew. Standing at the bus stop they could recognize Russians at a glance: their clothes were wrong. The men wore white nylon shirts, and grey polyester pants. The women were decked out in badly cut parodies of seventies designs. In contrast, the Bravermans felt themselves tuned up and equipped for anything. They had subdued but appropriate summer clothes, money in their wallets, a video camera. Their kids, unlike the pasty-faced Russian children, were lithe, tanned, and cool, in their hip 'Surfs-Up' T-shirts and neon-glow shorts. The Bravermans' wealth, their *health*, were embarrassing. It was hard not to feel superior.

'The Russians are what we might have been if our grandparents hadn't left,' said Nancy.

'I know,' Joel replied. 'They're like an earlier stage of Jew. Do you see their faces? It's strange, they're like old photographs.'

'They have gold teeth and moles on their faces,' Zachary chimed in. 'Why don't they have them removed, like at home?'

The Bravermans were ashamed to look at the Russians this way, as primitive, but try as they might they could not shake the feeling that, whenever they passed through the gate of the absorption centre, they entered a time warp.

One night the phone rang very late, past midnight. It was Oleg Krek, the downstairs neighbour. Joel had spoken to him once or twice, but the Russian's English was painful.

'Mr Joel,' the voice said, 'please help my ill son.'

'I'm sorry,' Joel replied, 'I'm not a doctor.'

'Yes,' said Oleg. 'They tell me Dr Braverman. At the desk.'

Joel suppressed a laugh – a child was sick. 'I'm not a doctor of medicine. I have a Ph.D. in computer science.'

There was silence for a moment, then Oleg said, 'Help please.' Joel went downstairs.

It took an hour to unravel the problem. The son, five-year-old Vadim, had a throat infection. A local doctor had prescribed antibiotics four days previously. The Kreks had not given the child the medicine because 'In Russia they do not give antibiotica.'

'I think,' Oleg had continued, 'Russia doctors better than here. Know more.'

Oleg's wife, Katya, scurried around making tea for Joel, bringing him little cakes, even offering him a damp flannel to wipe his forehead.

'Can you believe it?' Joel exclaimed to Nancy on his return. 'They were letting the kid suffer because they were afraid of the antibiotic. You know why they don't give "antibiotica" in Russia? Because they don't have any. No one can afford them!'

'They were just scared,' Nancy responded. 'They probably weren't familiar with the drug. I hope you didn't scold them.'

'I did,' said Joel, 'and I made them give the kid a dose while I watched.'

The Kreks needed more and more help from the Bravermans. Would Dr Braverman, as he was still an American citizen, write a letter in English to the US Embassy in Moscow requesting help in speeding up the visa process for Oleg's mother? Could Mrs Braverman watch the Krek children so that the parents could take English lessons along with their Hebrew lessons? Could the Bravermans lend their camera, video camera, food processor and, for one night only that stretched into a week, their television ('There is special show in Russian') to the Kreks? The Bravermans were happy to be of assistance. Even though they were newcomers themselves, they knew that they *owed* these Russian Jews something, and part of the pleasure of changing their own lives was this fresh demand that they help others. In addition to the borrowing and the baby-sitting, in three months Joel had loaned the Kreks, well, given them, about three hundred dollars – no big deal.

In the Ulpan, where the new immigrants learned Hebrew together, the Russians struggled. Joel and Nancy, relaxed and enthusiastic, took a warm bath in the new language, laughing and punning along with the teacher. In the packed bus on the way home, as the sweaty crowd pushed and shoved for position, the Bravermans tried to talk Hebrew to each other. They felt as though they were on a first date, nervously, excitedly groping for the appropriate words. The Russians stood sullenly, gripping the hand rails, swaying as the bus lurched round corners. They stared out of the windows and did not speak. If an Arab passenger approached them down the aisle, they moved away.

'They're racists,' Zachary had told Joel. 'They keep asking me about black people in America, and how near they lived to where we lived.'

'They're just curious,' Joel had replied, but the bus journeys were beginning to make him wonder.

From time to time, Joel and Nancy needed to indulge themselves. After all, they had not chosen Israel as a land of deprivation, a hair shirt to wear in penance for the easy lives they had led back home. At weekends, Joel would pay a special fee and take the family to the pool at the King David Hotel. There he could witness the world he had left behind, disguised as a tourist, and also enjoy the swimming. If the Bravermans turned in their chairs at the grass fringe of the pool they could look out over Mount Zion and the crenellated walls of the Old City. But mostly they kept their backs to the harsh beauty of that shuttered, hostile square mile, and concentrated instead on the bright splashing in front of them.

By late afternoon, the pool area was almost empty. A susurrant breeze blew through the pines and pistachio oaks around the hotel. Next to Joel, a father, an American (like himself?) was cutting deals with his son.

'Ten minutes out of the water then ten minutes in.'

'Five out, fifteen in.'

'Ten out, fifteen in.'

'Why can't I go in now?'

The father looked to the empty pool for an answer. 'The water's resting,' he replied. 'Can't you see that?'

Was Joel sorry that, unlike these itinerants, he would not be flying back to New York or L.A. or Boston? Not so far. Sometimes at dusk he looked out from his balcony in Beit Canada toward the Arab village of Sur Bahir. In the not-so-distant valley he could make out the village's minaret. The cries of the muezzin crackled nasally through loudspeakers, then drifted across to Joel in softer echoes. Sometimes there were calls to prayer, sometimes to stone-throwing. It seemed so strange. But was it really any different from hearing church bells ringing at home? True, people coming home from church didn't pelt your windshield with rocks. What did they pelt you with? Indifference? Immediately, Joel felt mean-spirited. His gentile friends and neighbours in Brookline had never treated him with anything except, well, friendship and neighbourliness, and hardly any of them even went to church. So what was he thinking of? Only this: standing on the balcony as the light faded, listening to the music of his enemies, he felt inexplicably, groundlessly, at home. He realized that in a way he had no right to, despite being Jewish; no right, that is, in the sense that childhood confers rights of ownership over certain smells and sounds that can never be appropriated by an expatriate adult. Nevertheless, he felt palpably that he had found the place where he was supposed to be.

Joel's reverie was interrupted by Nancy nudging him in the side. 'Joel,' she said, 'listen, they're paging you.'

'Would Dr Joel Braverman please come to the lobby.'

In less than a second Joel had given a quick look around, made sure that his kids hadn't drowned without his noticing, remembered that both his parents were already dead, and concluded that whatever waited for him in the lobby couldn't be too bad. He took three steps towards the hotel before the 'doctor' that had preceded 'Braverman' penetrated, and he knew before he saw them standing by the desk that the Russians were waiting for him.

The whole family was there, Oleg, Katya, the two children and a grandma, a real *babushka* – gold teeth, wavy grey hair, roly-poly body in a loose black dress.

Joel couldn't remember which Krek she belonged to. The Russians were in their best sabbath clothes: clean, pressed white shirts and khaki shorts for the father and son, pretty print dresses with thin straps for mother and daughter. Under their arms each member of the family carried a rolled-up towel presumably with a swimsuit inside. 'We swim too?' asked Oleg. 'Looks nice.'

At least once a week Joel would receive a job offer. Company representatives from Tel Aviv and Haifa would come to court him. One day the military paid him a visit: two tall, handsome men in smart civilian suits. Perhaps Joel would consider computer work with them? There were special advantages. Nothing was spelt out but Joel's two sons and their futures were mentioned an awful lot. Had the promise of a safe army unit for his children been hidden somewhere in the conversation? The notion was almost irresistible.

When Joel described the meeting to Nancy she could hardly conceal her excitement. Nevertheless, she made an effort to appear subdued; she didn't want to pressure Joel. 'Well,' she said, 'perhaps you should give it some thought.'

'I came because of Iraq's missiles,' Joel replied. 'That doesn't mean I want to work on our side's.'

'Well, anyway,' Nancy offered, 'it's nice to be asked.'

That was true. Oleg Krek had been asked by no one. He too, as he told Joel, was an engineer: 'Water engineer.' In three months he had garnered a solitary interview, with a Tel Aviv oil company who needed someone to check for groundwater pollution around their gas stations. But the job had gone to a native-speaker, and Oleg had returned from his day in the big city baffled and defeated.

Was it Joel's fault that Oleg couldn't get a job? Of course not. But then, as Nancy kept repeating, it couldn't be easy for Oleg to see Joel turn down offer after offer simply because he needed more time to 'settle in'; especially when the Kreks, who really didn't have two pennies to rub together, were so desperate.

Matters between Joel and Nancy came to head over the car. Joel wanted to travel more. 'We've seen so little,' he argued. 'Jerusalem's a great city to walk around but what about the other places? We could take a drive to Tiberias. It's supposed to be beautiful at this time of year.'

Nancy, however, was insistent. 'We can't buy a car until we leave the absorption centre. I'd be ashamed to go zooming past those poor souls sweating it out at the bus stop. And anyway, you'd stop for everyone. I'm sure we'd wind up taking the Kreks *everywhere*.'

'Fuck the Kreks,' Joel yelled. 'I'm not their fucking keeper. If I want to get a car I'll get a car.' But he didn't, citing lack of availability of the model he wanted as the reason.

The New Year came, and Yom Kippur. Joel, coming out of temple (he was still a three-times-a-year Jew) was shocked to see children bicycling *en masse* around the empty streets of the city. 'They wait all year for this,' explained a father whom he spoke to. 'No cars.'

School started, and with it, trouble. Zachary, who spent the first nights of October bent double over a short-wave radio trying to pick up the World Series on the Voice of America, was disrupting classes. His Hebrew was very weak, said his teacher, and he was being a terrible nuisance, even by Israeli standards.

'You're acting like a spoiled brat,' Joel lectured his son. 'We're here and we're going to stay here. You might as well learn to like it.'

'Well, you don't have to worry,' said Zach, 'because as soon as I'm old enough I'm going home. And if you think you're going to get me in that goddamn army you're wrong.'

Zachary was not the only frustration in Joel's life. Suddenly, he had hit a rock with the language. He couldn't seem to get any further than a kind of 'get-along' Hebrew.

The news on television was incomprehensible to him. When he talked he felt slow, tied up. He began to think his English was deteriorating too; he felt sometimes as if he were speaking in translation. He still attended the Ulpan classes, but now it was a drag to be in school. Hadn't he spent enough of his life in the classroom? The teacher, who at first had been so warm and friendly, now seemed silly, childishly enthusiastic. Joel didn't want to sing any more songs.

Nancy, meanwhile, had made friends and seemed snugger and happier as the days went by. She had taken a job working in a low-level administrative position at Hebrew Union College, a rabbinical school whose students were almost all from America. She was always being invited to this or that person's house for coffee. Soon she had become one of a group of part-time working mothers. In the late afternoons they would pick up their kids from school, and then go swimming together at the local pool.

Joel did not want to admit to himself that he felt lonely, but he did. What was he going to do? He supposed he should get a job, but something was holding him back. What? Was his sense of commitment wavering? Did Zachary have a point about the army? His sons would grow up to wear uniforms, carry guns. Of course, he had known this before they came, but seeing was different. It was all too easy now to imagine Zach and Josh in olive-green outfits with M–16s slung over their shoulders. He pictured them, like the others he saw on his journeys around town, tired, no, exhausted, their heads bent forward to take in the coolness of a metal seat-back on a bus. Did he have the right? Everything that had been fun was turning back into struggle. Even sex, which when they first arrived had been the best he could remember – the kids called out to them from the other room to quieten down – had reverted to the familiar. He wasn't doing such a good job as a pioneer. Even the Kreks seemed to be getting on their feet. Oleg had been offered a job in Beersheva. The desert town was expanding to accommodate ninety thousand new Russian immigrants. There was all kinds of water engineering to be done there. Soon, the Russians would prepare to move.

One afternoon in late October, Joel decided to walk through the Old City. He had been warned not to: there had recently been a spate of knifings. But, after behaving for three months as if the walled square mile teeming with people were not there, Joel had begun to feel more and more drawn to the place. He convinced himself that he wasn't being foolhardy. The stabbing victims had been students from the local yeshivas, dressed in orthodox garb, recognizably 'the enemy'. Didn't he still look like an American tourist? With his fine fair hair and blond beard he didn't even resemble his own idea of a Jewish-American.

Joel entered through the Jaffa gate. The square before him was deserted. Soon, making his way down the main street of the bazaar, Joel saw why. The Palestinian stall-keepers, in accordance, he now remembered, with instructions from the leaders of the intifada, were closing up shop. Afternoon was strike time: heavy metal shutters shuddered and clanged into place. Joel was reminded of the noise made by automatic garage doors when they closed to sequester the shiny new cars of his quiet American suburb. Back in Brookline, of course, there was no army patrol, loaded down with walkie-talkies and automatic weapons, scrutinizing you as you ended your work day. Joel's only audience when he came home had been a few spacey kids stopping their ball game for a moment to let him pull into his driveway.

Joel stood for a few minutes and watched a young man in jeans and a T-shirt that said 'University of Colorado' slowly bolt and padlock his door. What an insolent dance he made of shutting up shop. He twisted his body in mock exertion, as if turning the key were beyond his strength. The soldiers approached, and, for a moment, Joel thought he saw fear on every face. Then the patrol moved on; the young man, whistling to himself, disappeared around a corner.

Further on, the open market abruptly became a closed souk. Turning a corner, Joel found himself spotlit in a beam emanating from a high, unglazed skylight. He saw himself as an illuminated figure in a dark painting by an old master and felt uncomfortable. When Nancy dragged him on museum tours he tried to make her speed through the rooms that housed 'masterpieces'. He was always happy and relieved when they emerged into the airy colourful twentieth century.

It was cool in the covered souk. Joel, rubbing his bare arms, lingered a moment to take in a wonderful blend of smells. What was the nature of the merchandise now hidden behind closed doors? He wished the spice stores, at least, had stayed open. Joel breathed deeply, then, suddenly feeling exposed and vulnerable in the heavenly light that was pouring onto his face, he took three quick steps into a dark corner of the alley. Nearby he heard the raised voices of men arguing. Or were they arguing? Joel wasn't sure. They seemed to be speaking a mixture of Arabic and Hebrew – bad, broken Hebrew, for even he could make out some of the conversation: 'How much?' 'Are you crazy?' 'Tonight?' 'What time?' 'Okay' 'Where?' Footsteps echoed, a figure approached Joel and, without glancing his way, walked on. It was Oleg.

'My God,' Joel muttered to himself. 'My Russian.' His Russian was quickly followed by two Palestinian men deep in conversation; their expressive hands fluttered like caged birds.

For another hour Joel wandered the narrow streets of the souk. At first he was cautious, stopping every now and then to look over his shoulder. Was there hostility on these empty streets? Assuredly. But Joel began to feel, perhaps because he had no idea where he was, that he could go anywhere. He walked freely, confidently, as he never would have done in the off-limits black neighbourhoods around Boston. He walked the stations of the cross along the Via Dolorosa, toured the cobblestone crescents of the poor, wound his way up stone stairways to emerge on some blue-domed rooftop where a family's wash stiffened on a line.

What was Oleg up to? Wasn't he an engineer? One day Zachary had said, 'All the Russian kids say their parents are engineers,' and Joel had replied, 'Well, a lot of them are.' Was there a groundwater problem in the Old City? Soon Joel would have a chance to find out. The Kreks were coming to dinner tonight. It was to be a celebration of Oleg's new job. Joel would tell Oleg that he had seen him, ask him what he had been doing with the Palestinians.

But Joel did no such thing. During the meal, Oleg, voluble and excited, dominated the conversation. In his months in Israel he had acquired a conversational English, full of off-rhythm American slang. Joel was at once proud of, and irritated by, Oleg's English. After all, hadn't he invested in the man? As soon as this thought crossed Joel's mind he realized, with a hint of shame, that Oleg had become his personal greenhorn. He was the man off the boat, the relative you wait for on the dock in your sharp city clothes; his roughness made you feel smooth, his awkwardness lent you grace, his fanaticism and excitement made you feel modest and even-tempered. As he learned English you were proud of his progress, and ashamed of his mistakes.

'I tell you,' Oleg was saying between noisily slurped mouthfuls of Nancy's vichyssoise, 'we had our asses screwed on so tight in Russia we didn't know what to do. No, no, no, Joel, you have no idea. You talk about anti-Semitism, you talk about hatred; where I worked if there were two Jews in a room they'd say "What? Are you opening a goddamit synagogue in here?" And then, on the way home, me, Katya, the kids from school. I'm telling you Joel, you too Nancy, things you never heard in your whole life. "Zhid," they're yelling at my kids, and that was just the beginning. Much worse. Believe me Joel. Forget Tolstoy, forget Chekhov, these are primitive people.'

From here the conversation turned to the bounties of Israel. Joel had never heard Oleg so enthralled and enthusiastic. He got a job, and, suddenly, he was a psalmist: everything in the Holy Land was glorious. The people were friendly – 'real people, Joel, not ghosts' – the weather was perfect, the language, well, that would come, and, above all, no one called his children names. As for the Arabs, 'What do I owe them, Joel? Tell me. Do I owe them something?'

But what had Oleg been doing in the Old City? During an interruption in his monologue, caused by Josh spilling orange juice all over the table, Joel thought to ask him. However, a sentence from Katya, who hadn't been able to get a word in while her husband spoke, brought him up short.

'Oleg was in Beersheva all day today, he thinks he has found us an apartment.'

'Yes,' Oleg quickly added. 'and with swimming pool. Can you believe that? Shared with other families, but still, a pool.'

Joel looked across at Nancy, but as she knew nothing – afraid that she would worry, Joel had not told her where *he* had been that afternoon – she returned his incredulous look with a blank stare. Later, in the shuffle of bodies as the table was cleared, Oleg drew Joel aside. He had a request. The move to Beersheva was turning out expensive. Was there a chance to borrow another three hundred? In dollars, of course. Joel, listening involuntarily to the activity in the kitchen, heard a small avalanche of crockery as the kids completed their perilous journey to the sink. Water gushed, the radio came on, his wife's voice rose and fell, and Joel, who liked to pay his bills on time, reached into his wallet for three of the five crisp, hundred-dollar notes that he always kept tucked under the picture of his sons.

That night, Joel did not so much sleep as skim over sleep. The familiar suburban surf that assisted drowsiness back home – waves of engine noise breaking in volume – was gone. Instead, Joel heard, or thought he heard, faint music rising up from the valley, the thrum, wail, and quaver of an Arabic song. But he was not soothed. Finally, unable to put the conundrum of Oleg from his mind, Joel gave up on rest and went to stand sentry duty at his bedroom window. The moon, low and full, looked like a great silver bowling ball he might pluck out of the sky and roll down the dry slopes spread out before him.

Around 2 am, Oleg appeared, skipping down the steps at the front of the building. Joel didn't hesitate, he pulled on a pair of jeans and a T-shirt, slipped into his glo-in-the-dark Nikes, and rushed out. Certain that Oleg was heading for the Old City, Joel ran in that general direction. Sure enough, after half a mile of jogging he came in sight of his quarry. Oleg, a briefcase in his right hand, was striding out toward Hebron Road. Joel slowed to Oleg's pace. The streets were deserted. Once, an army jeep heading towards town whooshed past; its headlights threw first Joel, then Oleg, into a yellow pool of light.

Outside the St Claire convent, Oleg stopped to tie his shoelaces. Joel, acting as he had seen people do in the movies, flattened himself against a wall. Holding himself still, head down, so that his face would not be illuminated, Joel became unhappily aware of the uselessness of luminous running shoes for night-time detective work. But Oleg did not look back.

After an hour's walking, the last ten minutes up the winding inclines of the 'Pope's road', Oleg entered the Old City through Zion gate. Joel followed, peering round each corner of the *lamed* shaped entrance to make sure

that he was not observed. What on earth was he doing?
He could be home in bed, in Brookline!

As he stepped through the well-paved streets of the
Jewish Quarter, past cream- and pink-tinged stone homes
glowing in the moonlight, Joel tried to put his thoughts
together. Despite all the community activity back home –
kids' soccer leagues, poker games, fun, jokey lunches
with his colleagues, weekend jaunts with neighbours and
friends – Joel had felt a space, an emptiness, no, a *loneliness*, in America. Why? He didn't know. Why had he
come to Israel? Why go to a war zone? You had to be
crazy. But then again, he had come *because* of a war. Did
he just want to be a part of the action? He saw the missiles
fall on Tel Aviv and he felt his grandfather's beard being
tugged. This was bad thinking, diaspora thinking, he saw
that now. Israel could take care of itself. It didn't need
him. But for some as-yet-unformulated reason, he needed
it. And what about Nancy? Perhaps the whole adventure
was an elaborate ruse to put some zing back into their sex
lives. Couldn't there have been a less arduous way to
spice things up? Porn-flicks, a bag of grass and a night in
a fancy downtown hotel, or, for a big splurge, a weekend
in Paris? But no, they had to emigrate to the Middle East.
'The motions of our soul are in vain.' Where had he read
that? And what about our bodies?

Oleg had reached the foot of a broad stairway. He
stopped and looked around. Joel ducked back into
shadow. They were no longer in the Jewish Quarter. The
architecture had dramatically changed: church spires and
minarets rose in silhouette against the starlit sky.

The narrow alleyway where the two immigrants stood
was poorly lit, and cluttered with discarded crates. A
rancid smell of rotting fruit and vegetables hung in the
warm night air. Oleg began to run up the steps, the noise
of his heels reverberating in the darkness. Joel, pursuing
the echoes, was led round corners up the endless stairway
to a thin wooden door in a wall. He pushed through,

wincing as the hinges squeaked, and emerged onto a wide rooftop.

Joel looked around in shock and wonder. He had been transported. But to where? Before him, scattered in disorderly pattern, were fifteen or twenty mud-huts. Little monastic cells, each with a window cut, as if with a cookie-cutter, in the shape of a crucifix. On a far corner of the roof, a tall, slender African man in long white robes was deep in conversation with Oleg. Soon, they were joined by two other men. The Palestinians he had seen earlier in the day?

Joel moved as close as he could, concealing himself at the side of one of the little huts. The moon emerged from behind a cloud. There, on the bone-white roof, was a small, neatly laid table of crime: brown slabs of hash in unwrapped silver paper, plastic bags of grass secured by yellow twists, dollars (his dollars?) bound in an elastic band.

Should he do something? Leap out from his hiding place and demand his money? Wrestle Oleg to the ground? Bash his stupid Russian head in the dust? Joel moved forward, but immediately he felt restrained, pulled back, as if he wore an oversized child's harness and someone was tugging on the reins. It wasn't fear that had him in its grasp, but some other force, a sense of trespass, violation, transgression. But of what? Joel wasn't sure. He surveyed the scene before him. He watched the money and the dope change hands. And suddenly he knew. He remembered. He was a young man standing on a street corner on New York's Lower East Side. He had come over from NYU to buy marijuana. There were three men then too. They laughed and joked around with him. Maybe they were armed. Joel's knees had shaken with fear. He looked now. Yes, Oleg was shaking, his whole body was shaking. Let him go. Let it go. Joel turned back toward the stairway. He felt light-headed, dizzy. High above the

Old City, a shooting star exploded across the sky and fell into deep blackness.

After a day of silence about his night-time escapade, Joel knew that it was time to tell Nancy. He spent a morning doing errands in the city – groceries, the bank, the post office – then came home with the story on his lips. Approaching Beit Canada he saw Nancy sitting on the steps outside. Zachary was kicking a soccer ball against a brick wall with what seemed like unnecessary, but controlled, ferocity. As Joel approached, Nancy said, 'The Russians have moved.'

Joel looked at her; her face was white. 'How come they didn't say goodbye?'

'Because they moved our stuff with them.' Zachary's voice was thick with resentment. He unleashed a final vicious kick that sent his ball arching towards the brown scrubland at the side of the absorption centre. Joel rushed past him. Instead of waiting for the elevator he took the emergency stairs two at a time up to their fourth-floor apartment.

The TV, the clock radio, Joel's lap-top computer, all were gone. The electric kettle was missing from the kitchen, and the food processor. Everything that could be unplugged had been taken, except for Joel's Interplak toothbrush still warming itself on a bathroom shelf. In the bedroom, the video camera had been removed from its hiding place in Joel and Nancy's clothes closet. The closet itself was empty. Joel rushed back into the sitting room, astonished to notice now what he had missed on his first pass: all the furniture was gone. All that is, save Nancy's yellow director's chair. Joel went to sit in it, if only to confirm its material presence. A handwritten note had been pinned to the canvas back; it read 'Gone to U.S.A.', and then, underlined twice, 'ALL WILL BE RETURNED'.

105 Neptune Boulevard,
Lynn, Mass.   12 September 1992
U.S.A. (!)

Dear Friends,
   Here we are. Katya has job working for real estate
company. Although with economy the way it is not
much doing right now. Children in school,
everything not so O.K. there. American kids very
violent and sometimes even a gun is shown. We don't
like this, want them to go to nearby Jewish school,
but many Russians here and not much scholarships.
O.K., what I did, I did for reasons. I was not
criminal. You do not know about hard lives in Russia.
I *am* water engineer. Downstairs, in lobby at night,
are the others, what you think I was. Even I afraid
to go down. The thing is to move to suburb. This
takes job – and money! So far, no luck. No hard
feelings. Israel not for us. Do you know story about
how Jews a long time ago got from Russia to Israel?
Boat pulls up in Haifa, someone yells 'New York'
and all dumb ones get off. Not true, Joel, of course,
not true, but I thought that you would like.
                    All best to your family.
                    Oleg

Jerusalem   October 30, 1992

Dear Oleg,
   My grandfather once said to me, 'You can't walk
on hot coals and not expect to get your feet burned.'
I walked, didn't I? You must have needed a big truck.
You must have kicked up a lot of red dust. I would
like the clock radio returned. It was a present to my
oldest son. He liked to listen to the Voice of America.

From Shanghai

The advice note, dropped on my father's desk in the first week of September 1955, lay unread for a week. My father was away from home, resolving a dispute over burial sites in Manchester. He was a synagogue troubleshooter, the Red Adair of Anglo-Jewish internecine struggles, and it was his job to travel up and down the country, mollifying rabbis and pacifying their sometimes rebellious congregations. It was only when he returned to his office in Tavistock Square that he learned that a package awaited him at London docks. My father was a little confused. The note had come from the Office of Refugee Affairs, a department, now almost defunct, that he had little to do with. What could possibly be sent to him, and why?

During his lunch hour he travelled to Tilbury, emerging by the loading dock on the river where bulky cargo vessels lined up beneath towering cranes. It took him a long time to locate the appropriate office, and even longer to find the right collection point. But my father was used to bureaucrats, and patient with them, and he chatted amiably while the papers he had brought with him were perused and stamped.

In the warehouse, he was presented not with the brown paper parcel that he had imagined but with two enormous crates, lowered to his feet by a man on a forklift truck.

'What's in them?' asked my father.

'No idea, guv. They're in off the boat from Shanghai.'

'I see,' said my father, utterly bemused. After the usual delays and indignation, a crowbar was provided, and my father, with the reluctant aid of the forklift driver, pried open one of the wood slats on the side of the crate. The driver, his inquisitiveness aroused, tore through some thin paper wrapping.

'Looks like books,' he said.

'Books?'

'Yes, mate, books.'

'But who from?'

They searched the surface of the crate; the bill of lading indicated only 'P.O. Box 1308, Shanghai'.

'Well, I've got work to do,' the driver announced, remounting his forklift and starting the engine.

My father reached into the crate and dislodged one of the books. It was a German translation of *The Collected Tales of Hans Andersen*, strongly bound in blue linen. He took out another book: it was written in a language he couldn't understand, Japanese or Chinese. The third book was, again, the *Collected Tales*, but this time in English. He tugged out five more illustrated English-language versions of *The Fairy Tales of Hans Andersen*. My father returned to the Far Eastern text and flicked through the pages. Sure enough, there were the tell-tale drawings: a duckling, a nightingale, three dogs with eyes as big as saucers.

Over the next few months more and more crates arrived, each one adding to the Andersen collection. My father arranged to have them held in a warehouse near the docks. My mother was less than pleased with the extra expense imposed upon our family by this storage of books from nowhere. After all, we had only recently been freed from the restrictions of wartime rationing: filling the larder was her priority, not the unasked-for freight of a phantom dispatch agent. But my father reacted in his usual lighthearted manner, as if we had all entered a fairy tale. From out of the blue a gift had come our way. Who could possibly guess what the magical consequences might be?

By the end of the year we had some twenty thousand books in storage. One winter morning, under a cold blue sky, my father took me down to the warehouse with him to view the crates. It was like a trip to the pyramids. I ventured cautiously into the dark alleyways between the wood containers, piled three high, as if these mysterious monuments held an ancient power. What on earth had we come to possess? Of course, my father had written to the P. O. Box in Shanghai, but so far he had received no reply.

As we walked away from the docks, the ships grew smaller and smaller in the distance, until they looked like the curios at the fun fair that you could snatch up with the metal jaws of a miniature crane. I asked my father, as I had heard my mother ask him in a moment of frustration and anger, why we didn't sell the books. 'Because they are not ours to sell,' he replied.

It was Sunday, and we were both free, for the only day of the week, from the dual constraints of work (homework in my case) and synagogue. We walked all the way to Tower Bridge. A small crowd had gathered in an open area on the wharf. Nearby, on the river, a brightly painted houseboat, *The Artful Dodger*, had been moored.

A small, muscular man, with a shaved head and an ugly tattoo inscribed upon his forearm – barbed wire entwining a naked woman – was passing round a set of heavy chains for the crowd to inspect. Shortly he bound himself up. My father, who appeared more captivated than most, was selected to turn, and then pocket, the key of a massive padlock that secured our escapologist. The Artful Dodger then asked my father to gag him. After this a giggling woman from the audience helped the escapologist step into a burlap sack, laid out on the flagstone next to him. This accomplished, the woman waved to her cheering friends, and tightened the drawstring with a flourish.

Behind the writhing sack, the black Thames flowed hastily. Two swift Sunday-morning scullers, who had taken my attention, disappeared behind a chugging tugboat. By the time they emerged, our prisoner was free. I wasn't surprised. I knew his trick. I had read all about Houdini in a school library book. I knew that our man had swallowed a duplicate key before the show, and then regurgitated it while in the sack. But, to my astonishment, I found myself no less impressed. Escape, however it was accomplished, was the glittering thing.

In the spring, my Uncle Hugo arrived from Shanghai. He wasn't really my uncle but my father's second cousin. He brought with him his wife, Lotte, and nothing more than the clothes on their backs. At first, of course, he was simply a stranger who walked into my father's office one day in March, and announced that he had come to claim both the Andersen books and a relationship.

My father took Hugo for lunch, by which I mean that they went to a nearby park, sat on a bench, and shared sandwiches. It was one of those transitional spring days, when it is warm enough in the sun but still very cold in the shade. While they sat, side by side, lifting their faces to the pale medallion in the sky, Hugo told his story. He had been expelled from his home in the Austrian Burgenland in 1938. Like many others he had fled, in desperation, to the International Settlement in Shanghai, the only city in the world he could enter without a visa. A gentile friend, Artur Jelinek, a philatelist, had forwarded the Andersen books to China with money left for the purpose by Hugo. He had lived in Shanghai for fifteen years, working as a technician in a hospital laboratory. By profession he was a biologist, he had written a botanical treatise on mushrooms; by inclination he was a bibliophile. In Austria, before the war, through penny-pinching, perseverance and resourcefulness, he had accumulated what he believed to be the world's second largest collection of Hans Andersen books, exceeded only by the corpus owned by the Danish royal family.

My father listened. There had been, of course, a thousand refugee stories in wide circulation in the London

Jewish community in the previous ten years; most reported greater hardship, some less. Hugo had escaped early. He was lucky. Of course, his life had been terribly disrupted, but he was alive, he was here, his collection was intact.

'But how did you get to me?' my father asked.

'Your cousin, Miki, the one who . . .'

My father nodded before Hugo could proceed. He already knew the details, and wanted to spare himself the pain of hearing them repeated.

'Well,' Hugo continued, 'Before – that is, some months before – he was taken, when I was about to leave, he gave me your name. He told me that you were an administrator for Jews. The address of the office I discovered in Shanghai.'

'But why,' my father continued, 'didn't you reply to my letters?'

'Arthritis,' Hugo replied, and held his misshapen hands out for my father to inspect. 'I cannot hold a pen.'

'But surely . . .' my father stopped. Sometimes, he told me later, an excuse, given for whatever reason, simply has to be accepted.

Hugo had met Lotte in Shanghai. Like him she was a refugee from Hitler's Europe. But, unlike him, she was vivacious and energetic. Partly this derived from the fact that she was twenty years Hugo's junior. Although Hugo was only in his mid-fifties, he was, to my eyes, an old man, with his shock of white hair and deeply lined face. It was Lotte who enchanted me. She would arrive for Saturday-night dinner in a fox-fur stole (borrowed from her neighbour) and chain-smoke through a long cigarette holder. She liked to sing, and after supper she would call my father to the upright piano in our dining room. He would accompany her in feisty, throaty renditions of songs in German that I couldn't understand, but of which both Hugo and my mother appeared to disapprove. I would like to stand near Lotte, in the aura of her rich heavy perfume, and take deep breaths.

Lotte's family, miraculously, had survived the war and were now dispersed all over the world. Her parents were in America with her sister, Grete; one of her brothers was in Buenos Aires, the other in Israel. Sometimes she would bring me the latest postcards and letters that she had received, and together we would sit in the kitchen, soak the stamps off, and carefully catalogue them in my album. You might have thought that this kind of activity would have been more up Hugo's street, but he remained remarkably indifferent to me, almost cold, until the day that my father gave me the present.

Two evenings a week my father took art classes at the Adult Education programme of St Martin's School of Art. The works that he produced provoked a great deal of hilarity in our household. He generally painted nudes. The teacher, not rich in imagination, seemed to demand two poses of his models. The first a dull, straightforward, upright-seated position in a high-backed chair; the second, a 'sensual', provocative draping of the body over a velvet-backed chaise longue. My father, an admirer of Matisse but not a great colourist himself, would bring home to us strange light-brown figures, twisted, not altogether intentionally, into expressionist poses. He would line his canvases up against a wall in the hall. My brother and I would collapse in laughter. My mother, busy with supper, barely gave the works more than a passing glance. To his credit, my father took our cruel responses very well. For two nights a week he seemed to enjoy playing the part, not of the overburdened synagogue administrator, but of the lonely artist struggling in a hostile, philistine world.

Perhaps in order to establish for himself evidence of the duality of his personality, or perhaps, in some unconscious way, to sanctify the graven images that he created, my father initialled all his paintings in the bottom right-hand corner, but with *Hebrew* letters: a serpentine *lamed* and squarish *vav* that served to represent the artist, Leslie Visser.

After the arrival of Hugo and Lotte, I thought I began to detect something new in 'Lamed Vav's' paintings (my brother and I had taken up the initials as sobriquet). I may have been mistaken, but it seemed to me that the faces of the nudes were coming more and more to carry Lotte's features: her full lips and unmistakable green eyes. But whether this was the result of my fantasies or those of 'Lamed Vav' has never been clear to me.

My father had a friend at the art class, a man named Joe Kline, who worked as a salesman for the publishing company of Eyre & Spottiswoode. One night, my father came home with a small cardboard box packed with four hardback books. 'More?' said my mother, who was suspicious of all transactions involving bound volumes. We were still defraying the costs of the Andersen storage until Hugo and Lotte could 'get on their feet'.

'These are a gift,' my father responded, 'from Joe. They're remainders, out of print, but in mint condition. It was really very nice of him. There's a book for every member of our family, including you.'

There was a novel for my mother, while my brother received a How-to guide to safe chemistry experiments in the home. My book was, well, a brand new, very nicely illustrated edition of *The Collected Tales of Hans Andersen*. 'Coals to Newcastle,' said my mother scornfully.

I was twelve, a little old for Hans Andersen, I thought, although secretly I still liked the stories and soon became quite attached to one lavish illustration in particular. It showed the beautiful princess from 'The Tinder Box', asleep on the giant dog's back, a low-cut dress revealing the cleavage of what the illustrator had decided would be disproportionately large breasts. This colour print fed into the fantasy connected to Evelyn, the fourteen-year-old girl whose bedroom window faced mine across the two postage-stamp-sized lawns that abutted our homes. Recently, I had removed a round mirror from my bicycle, bolted it to a long stick, and attached it to one of my bedposts. In this way I was able to watch Evelyn Boone undress in her room, without being observed myself. Unfortunately, most of the time, Evelyn took what was the conventional precaution in our enclosed neighbourhood of drawing the curtains before disrobing. So far, I had not seen any more in my magic mirror than had already been granted to me by Eyre & Spottiswoode's dubiously inspired illustrator.

From the first time he laid eyes upon it Uncle Hugo wanted my book. In the wide world of desire, there is little that exceeds the covetousness of the collector. From a distant, unconcerned relative, Hugo suddenly transformed into a charming, wily confrère. I was not immune to the bribery and seductiveness of adults, nor was I invulnerable to the parental cajoling that began when my father (my mild-mannered father!) decided to join in the fray and persuade me to hand over my book to Hugo. Indeed, I might have given in, were it not for the fact that what Hugo was asking for constituted, however bizarrely, a piece of the puzzle of my erotic life, one that I was unwilling to relinquish. Lotte, who seemed to have a sense that there was more than stubbornness and obstinacy to my refusal, took my side.

'You don't have enough books?' she asked her husband. 'So you have to steal from a child?'

'It's not stealing,' my father interposed. 'Hugo has offered Michael an extremely rare and valuable first edition in return for his book. We are talking about a swap here. An exchange in which Michael will come out the winner.'

The two men pressured me for a month, but I held my ground.

'Why can't he buy the book from someone else, if he

wants it that badly?' I whined to my father, after Hugo
had left the house one day.

'Because it is unavailable in bookshops, and Uncle Hugo
does not steal from libraries. What is more, buying books
costs money, and, at the moment, Hugo and Lotte are
trying to *save* money. You're not too young to understand
that. Joe Kline tells me that they only printed a thousand
copies of your edition. It didn't do well. Too many com-
petitors on the market. It isn't valuable, but Hugo would
have an impossible job tracking one down. To you, it's
virtually worthless, but to Hugo, as part of a collection,
it means something. Has it sunk in what Hugo is offering
you in return? You could own a book worth, maybe, fifty
pounds!'

Fifty pounds to give up Evelyn Boone's breasts? For,
yes, I could no longer distinguish her teenage bumps from
the more developed forms that belonged to the princess
in the illustration. Out of the question!

For reasons of domestic propriety (perhaps my mother
had noticed the Lotte heads on the naked bodies too) the
Wassermans had, some time during the summer, been
switched from Saturday nights to Sunday afternoons.
Hugo and Lotte had bought a car on the HP, an old
Singer with seventy thousand miles on the clock. In this
distinguished vehicle, Hugo at the wheel, Lotte making
hand signals because the left indicator did not work, they
negotiated a slow, careful way to our house each week-
end. When they pulled up at the kerb my father would
look out of the window and say, 'Here comes the Rolls
Canardly, rolls down one side of a hill, can 'ardly get up
the other.'

Hugo was now a fully incorporated member of something my father called the 'Cheese-Cake Club'. This
organization now boasted four members, men from the
neighbourhood who gathered weekly to overpraise my
mother's pâtisserie and discuss the contemporary scene.
One of the men, Sidney Oberman, would arrive with the

week's newspapers under his arm. It was his responsibility to select and underline topics for further discussion. The group's heroes were Winston Churchill, the late Chaim Weizman, and Dr Armand Kalinowski a brilliant Jewish panellist on the popular radio show *Brains Trust*. In deference to this invisible mentor, the members of the 'Cheese-Cake Club' each sported a bow-tie, symbol of decorum and high thought.

Six weeks after Hugo had first held my book in his hands for examination and quiet evaluation, the Wassermans arrived, as usual, late for Sunday tea, and, as usual, in the middle of an argument. The general cause of their altercations was 'The Collection'. The Wassermans were poor. They lived in a tiny two-room flat in Willesden Green. Hugo had looked for laboratory work, but, he said, his strong German accent made prospective employers uneasy. The Wassermans' small income accrued from Lotte's piano lessons offered to neighbourhood children in their own homes, and from piece-work (advice on fungus and fungicides) that Hugo performed as assistant to a local landscape gardener. According to Lotte, if Hugo were only to sell his books, they could live like royalty. On the other hand, if Hugo ever tried to unpack his books in her home, he would have to find another wife.

Lotte's scorn for Hans Christian Andersen and his work knew no limits. Fairy tales! What nonsense. A collection of Goethe or Tolstoy she might respect, although, in her present crisis, she would still want to sell it. But a grown man straining his eyes poring over 'The Emperor's New Clothes' in twenty different languages? What a terrible waste.

When Lotte spoke this way Hugo flushed deeply; he would look around to see if my brother or I were in earshot. When his eyes met ours we would try to look distracted and hard of hearing. On this particular occasion, their argument appeared to have peaked shortly before the ring on our doorbell, and what I overheard as

I opened the door ('You want us to remain poor all our lives?'/'Is this all you care about, money?') were their last tired shots, the blows of a boxer whose arms are spent, and legs wobbly.

Lotte moved shakily toward the kitchen. 'I need a glass of water,' she said. Hugo carefully removed his jacket and searched our hall cupboard for a hanger. Were there tears in his eyes? I wasn't sure, but suddenly I felt sorry for him. Perhaps it was the look of deep exhaustion on his face (a look I had seen before but not really registered) that softened me, or maybe it was simply the fact that, for the first time since we had begun our battle of wills, he did not say to me, 'So, have you changed your mind?' Whatever the reason, I hovered around until Hugo had hung up his jacket, and then I said, 'I'll swap.'

The ceremonial exchange of books did not take place for more than a fortnight. It was mid-August, and time for our annual holiday. My parents would book us into some quiet, respectable boarding house in Margate or Swanage or Southbourne, making sure to order vegetarian meals in advance, in this way anticipating and surmounting problems that might arise with *kashrut*. Off we would go, packed snugly into our old Ford Prefect. After a long eighty miles or so of traffic jams, car-sickness and back-seat fights, we would arrive at someone else's house, not too different from our own, ready to read indoors while the rain fell in sheets; play crazy-golf in light drizzle; and venture out on the three or four fine, warm days that nature seemed to guarantee us, to swim in the cold sea and shiver.

This year, however, we were doing something different. We had *rented* a seaman's cottage on the beach in Folkestone. High, choppy waves thundered against the retaining wall behind the little dwelling. When I lay in bed at night I felt as if my bedroom were a ship's cabin, pitching and rolling in the summer winds. In the mornings, my brother and I explored the dunes near where the ferry came in from Boulogne. The sandy knolls and hillocks were still dotted with concrete pill-boxes. We clambered inside these dry chambers, peered through their narrow window slits, and pretended to be gunners scanning the Channel for approaching German aircraft.

At the end of the first week my father was suddenly and mysteriously called back to London. All we knew was that Lotte had phoned one day in a state of high excitement. My father had a few whispering sessions with my mother. But, after he had departed, she claimed, and she seemed to be telling the truth, that my father had told her only that Hugo and Lotte had a real emergency, not of a medical nature, but serious enough to warrant his returning home for a couple of days to help them out.

It rained for the duration of my father's three-day absence. We visited a shop that held demonstrations in toffee manufacture, went to the pictures to see Danny Kaye in *The Court Jester*, and attended a children's talent contest in the local town hall.

When he returned, late one night, my father appeared anxious and disturbed. In fact, he was so agitated that I allowed myself to imagine, for one brief flicker of a thought, that he and Lotte had perhaps, well . . . no, it was inconceivable.

The Prince of Denmark, we learned eventually, had sent an emissary to Hugo. The royal family's librarian wished to review the collection. There was genuine interest from Copenhagen. If Hugo would not agree to sell it whole, perhaps he would permit the collection to be split up?

Lotte had called on my father to help her persuade Hugo that this was a once-in-a-lifetime chance. They could escape their dreary lodgings and dead-end jobs. They could move to Golders Green, better, to Hampstead! If he wished to pursue his 'hobby', Hugo could open an antiquarian bookshop. My father had spoken to Hugo, but he was powerfully resistant to the idea of selling.

'Leslie, you don't understand,' he had said. 'I have to hold it together. The collection has to be protected.'

But then something happened. Here, my father paused in his narrative, as if to gather strength. My mother poured him a cup of tea. Hugo had received a letter in the post. He had not let Lotte see it, but after reading it he had rushed out of the house. He had gone missing for a day and a night, and when he returned in the early hours of this morning, hatless, soaked through, with his teeth chattering, he had simply slumped in a chair and refused to explain himself. My father had visited the Wassermans for lunch. Hugo had been polite, but withdrawn. He did not want to discuss the collection any more. Perhaps, after all, he would sell, he only wanted to be left alone and given a little more 'time to think'.

'Well,' said my mother testily, when my father had finished speaking. 'I think they've got a nerve. Interrupting a person's holiday, and then behaving in this outrageous fashion, when you – and only *you* would do this – went up there to help them.' My father didn't reply. Outside the sea swelled and surged, spraying droplets of surf against our kitchen windows. I thought, in my ignorance, that my mother had a point.

When we returned to London, my father immediately had to deal with a crisis at work: for the first time, a woman had been elected to the Board of Management of a North London synagogue, and now the entire spiritual staff, rabbi, cantor, beadle and choirmaster, were threatening to resign. 'This is the beginning of the end for Judaism,' the rabbi had written back to headquarters, and added in parentheses, ' "A foolish woman is clamorous: she is simple, and knoweth nothing." (Proverbs 9:13)' My father was dispatched to calm everybody down.

The school holidays were drawing to a close. I had to buy a new blazer, and stock up on those sweet-smelling essentials, an eraser, a new exercise book, blue-black ink, and a fountain pen. In the subdued excitements of anticipation before a new school year, I almost forgot about Hugo and Lotte.

One evening, when an autumn chill could already be felt in the air, they turned up on our doorstep. Lotte was transformed. She was wearing a white crepe de chine blouse, and a knee-length black satin skirt. Her hair was dressed in a chic new style. She was brimming over with joy. 'He's going to sell!' she announced even before she greeted us.

Hugo followed her sheepishly into the house. It seemed that Lotte had jumped the gun. Her emphatic expectation of great wealth had led her to spend, in one brave day, the little savings that they had managed to accumulate in the previous six months of struggle and hardship. 'Yes, I will sell,' said Hugo. 'But who knows what I will get?'

Late in the evening Hugo pulled me aside. 'Come in the other room', he said. 'We need to talk.' I had been expecting him to approach me, and wondering why he had delayed. 'Listen,' he whispered, pushing his face close to mine. I smelled alcohol on his heavy breath. 'I am going to give you a book. I don't want *them* to get it. It's very valuable, but it's worth nothing. I want you to keep it. You can't sell it.'

The bars of our electric fire, turned on for the first time in four months, glowed bright orange and gave off a pungent scent of burned dust. Hugo raked his white hair back with his fingers. 'You must,' he said, taking me by the shoulders, 'you, above all people, must forgive me.' Despite the heat that was moving in waves up my back, I felt a chill go through me. He was weeping now, sobbing, his shoulders heaving as if he could never stop. Suddenly, Lotte and my father appeared in the doorway. They rushed to Hugo, put their arms around him, and led him back into the kitchen.

That night, my parents sent my brother and me to bed early. But, as was our custom when this happened, we crept half-way down the stairs to eavesdrop on the grown-up conversation. We sat in our pyjamas, hugging the banister. In the brightly-lit kitchen, Hugo began to speak, in low tones, and with a halting voice. At first we only caught words and phrases: 'wife', 'son', 'arrangements', 'waited and waited', 'betrayed', 'not even Lotte'. Huddled on the stairs we heard, clear as train whistles in the night, sharp intakes of breath around the kitchen table. Soon we grew used to Hugo's broken, hoarse whisper.

If, at any point in Hugo's story, my brother and I could have returned to our beds, we would probably have done so. But curiosity had called us to listen, and now we were trapped.

After ten or fifteen minutes Hugo paused for a moment. My father got up and switched the lights off in the kitchen. It was a strange thing to do. Perhaps he wanted to take the harsh light of self-interrogation off Hugo. Now, Hugo's voice came up to us out of darkness. 'The collection,' he said, 'the collection came to Shanghai, but not my family.' There was a long silence. 'Soon after the war, I received a confirmation. My wife. Someone from the woman's camp who was there. I received a letter. But my son, of course, unlikely, all right impossible, but even so. Two weeks ago, a letter comes. You know. Sixteen years. An official letter; the place, the date.' Hugo began a muffled sob. 'My Hans, Hans Wasserman, Hans Wasserman.' He said the name again and again.

It was thirty years before I opened the edition of the *Collected Tales* that Hugo had given me. My nine-year-old son's teacher had invited parents to come to school and share their favourite children's story with the Nintendo-obsessed throng. I thought for a while before settling (of course!) on Andersen's 'The Tinder Box'. My old, illustrated copy of the tales had long since been lost in some chaotic transfer from home to home. But I had managed to hold onto Hugo's gift. It was an ordinary-looking book, with a slightly torn blue binding and faded gold lettering on the cover. The early pages were spotted with brown stains. The frontispiece proudly announced 'A New Translation, by Mrs H. B. Paull'. I flicked through the pages; they appeared unmarked. I turned to the Contents: a faint circle had been inscribed around 'The Brave Tin Soldier'. I found the story, and read it through. In the last sentence two phrases had been thinly underlined in pencil: 'instantly in flames', 'burnt to a cinder'.

Schoom

A few months ago I was taken by a friend to the archaeological dig in the Beit She'an Valley. It was a warm summer morning. I had emerged unusually depressed from my therapy session with Dr Schoom, but the anticipation of seeing the excavated city-fortress of Yodfat cheered me up. For two weeks only, the ruins of two-thousand-year-old streets and buildings were to be open to a variety of foreign specialists, but not to the public (the fear of damage was too great); after this, the site would be covered and closed.

My companion, Avital Lorch, had been working on the dig for about eighteen months, and sleeping with me for about half that time. Lately, things hadn't been going too well in our relationship, on account of my philandering. I hadn't *cheated* – we weren't married – and as I explained to Avital, she was away a lot at the dig. But neither she nor Dr Schoom was impressed by my lame excuses. Schoom, of course, wanted to get to the bottom of my inconsistency. Avital didn't care why I had gone to bed with the waitress from The Little Souperie, or the art student, or the daughter of the cleaning woman (who had substituted for her mother one happy, fateful day), but she did think enough was enough. 'Don't be a fool,' she said. 'Don't blow a good thing. Control yourself.'

I might have mastered my desires better if Schoom hadn't kept falling asleep. I would be halfway through a session when he would start to nod off. It didn't matter that I was describing intense or dramatic moments – my father keeling over at my feet when I was nine, or Susan Cranston, my sister's best friend, slowly unzipping my fly and reaching into my pants when I was thirteen – his eyes would begin to glaze over, he would stifle a yawn, and soon enough, head thrown back and breathing deeply, he was gone. I would wait a few moments and then cough, or call 'Dr Schoom, Dr Schoom.' He would come to with a start. 'Are you all right?' I would ask. He would inevitably reply, 'What are you talking about?' and pretend that he hadn't missed a beat.

So I started to think that I was having affairs in order to keep Schoom awake: to give him something juicy to look forward to in my sessions. I told him as much. 'I don't want to bore you,' I said, 'so I'm trying to lead an interesting life.'

'Ah yes,' he replied, 'the middle child desperate for his parents' attention, afraid that it is somewhere else.'

'Well,' I said, 'you have seemed *distracted* recently.'

'Not at all,' he responded, 'although your little joke with me may not be so far off the mark. What *do* all these love affairs have to do with me? Why can't you seem to spend a single night alone? And why do you feel so strongly the need to entertain me?'

'You tell me,' I said.

'No,' he replied, '*you* tell *me*.'

I tried another tack. 'Could it be,' I conjectured, 'that I'm very attracted to women?'

Schoom tilted his ancient head, with its monk-like fringe of white hair, so that he was now viewing me almost sideways. 'Do you really believe that?' he asked. Time was up.

One morning I arrived ten minutes early for my appointment. Oddly, the door to Schoom's office was minutely ajar. I heard a young woman's voice say, 'And what's more, it's like a dungeon in here,' and then she emerged, walking past me, where I sat in a canvas butterfly chair, without glancing my way. But I saw her: short brown hair, green eyes, ever so pretty, but hard too, with a purposeful stride, and a tuned-up body. 'Bet he doesn't fall asleep with her,' I thought.

So I had the Schoom problem and the fidelity problem, and somehow I was to understand they were linked. Never mind that on this morning's drive out of Jerusalem I was transported, as was so often the case, by the dusty blue light over the hills, the warm breeze, and some dizzying, mingled scent – petroleum and almond. 'Let's stop in on my cousin,' I said to Avital. 'We need coffee.'

My cousin Ruthie lived on Kibbutz Hakarosh, which had been founded in the mid-sixties by young immigrants from the Upper West Side—Jewish Left. These intellectual hippies were now fully-fledged, ideologically strict kibbutzniks. No member of Hakarosh was allowed a VCR in their home; and when Ruthie's daughter, Noa, wanted to get contact lenses because she thought glasses made her look ugly, the kibbutz held a meeting and voted not to let her. Ruthie was a lover of socialist constraint, but even she had hoped that her daughter would prevail.

Avital turned off at the Sha'ar Hagai junction and we were soon sitting on the veranda of Ruthie's little bungalow sipping *botz* (which is coffee named after mud) with one of Ruthie's neighbours. When my cousin finally showed up she was dressed in Bedouin clothes and accompanied by an old man, also in Bedouin outfit.

'Hello,' I said. 'Purim was two months ago, what's with the getup?'

'Oh no,' she said, 'my luck. You.'

Ruth was not a frivolous person, and she thought I was. Nevertheless she patiently offered me an explanation. The kibbutz grew olives but the pressing was done on the West Bank. She always went and oversaw the process, but now it was unsafe for her to go *as herself*. Her Bedouin partners, with whom the kibbutz split the profits, had arranged for her to be accompanied to the Arab town of Ramallah, but in disguise. 'Look,' she said, 'Arafat was once smuggled out of Jordan as a woman, and nobody spotted him; I can certainly make it.'

This deception reminded me of my second Schoom problem. My therapist wanted me to steal something for him, and that was why I had been particularly done in after the morning session. I told him where I was going and with whom, and he woke right up. 'Listen,' he said, 'can you bring something back for me? You know I am a collector.' I did know. His office was filled with artefacts: pottery shards, ancient utensils, slivers of Roman glass.

'I'm an American economist,' I said, 'not a thief. I came here two years ago to advise the Israeli government, not to steal from it.'

'Don't be ridiculous,' he said. 'You are a reactive depressive with an overdeveloped libido.' In eighteen months this was the first diagnosis he had offered me.

He was very agitated. 'Look,' he said, relenting a little. 'I'm not asking you to plunder the graves of the pharaohs; a memento is all I request. You know very well that the site is to be closed. Bring something from the ground. What will it matter? The government, quite rightly, is going to let the city lie dormant for eternity. All we laymen shall have then is our photographs. *You* have been offered a great gift. You are going to be in *the place*. If you could return to me just a fraction of that gift, in the form of an earthenware fragment. Really, is that such a big deal?

I didn't make Schoom any promises. I thought I'd see how things panned out. At Ruthie's place, where the veranda roof had been constructed out of old orange crates and there was absolutely nothing worth swiping, we lingered a while over our coffee. Ruth told me that when we were kids she hated coming to my house because my parents always made her take her shoes off so that our rugs wouldn't get damaged. Then she told me that I used to sweat out of the pores at the sides of my nostrils every time I ate a certain type of candy. Who needed to hear this stuff? Why dredge up the details?

What did it lead to? Who did it help? In the distance, a tractor laboriously made its way up the side of a steep hill, pulling a heavy load. 'There goes David with the cow fodder,' said Ruth.

Meanwhile, Avital had been describing the Beit She'an excavations to Dorit, the neighbour, and Farhad, the Bedouin. They had uncovered, she said, along with the usual arrowheads and coins, the remains of a pottery! The prized discovery was a set of intact oil lamps made from moulds in the Middle-Roman period. Almost two thousand years ago, for the first time, because of a new technique, ancient Palestinian potters had been able to depict a variety of raised designs on the upper surface of the lamps. The results were stunning. There were representations of Torah shrines, an amphora within an arch, decorative grape patterns, and, most unusually, what looked like a reclining figure (although it couldn't be) with its head resting on the pinched spout set for a wick. Dorit wanted to know more; Farhad gazed around as if nothing that was being said could possibly have anything to do with him.

Two men in blue work shirts began to approach us down the winding dirt path that led to Ruthie's house. 'Okay,' I said to Avital. 'Time to go.'

'Excuse me, Daniel, but I'm in the middle of a conversation.' I always got a little nervous on the kibbutz. I had this feeling that if you stayed too long someone would come and get you to work. One minute you could be relaxing with a relative, the next minute it was *you* dragging the cow food up the hill. Avital talked a while longer while I watched the work-shirt men until they were safely out of sight.

After a while, we got up and walked across a cracked-cement basketball court to our car. Avital turned the key in the ignition and waved goodbye to Ruthie. 'Hold up,' I said. I was a little worried about my cousin, and decided to tell her so. I leaned out of the window. 'You're all I've got in this country,' I said. 'I don't think you should play dress-up in the Occupied Territories.'

Ruthie raised the long, richly embroidered sleeve of her Bedouin dress, and gave me the finger. 'Drive on,' I said to Avital.

The sun was high and strong as we crossed the valley toward the site. I looked at Avital dexterously manoeuvring the car around tight curves and down narrow lanes. When she turned her head the three stud earrings that she wore in her right ear caught the sun and sparkled. What a smart, beautiful woman she was. So why the need for the others? The truth was, I knew the answer. I wanted to be enlightened. I slept with other women because I was fascinated by their stories. Don't get me wrong, the sex mattered – sometimes it was great and sometimes it wasn't – but what I especially cherished were certain moments of intimacy, lying in bed afterward, listening. It always amazed me how people who were strangers a week, a day, or even a couple of hours earlier, would reveal their most secret thoughts after making love. For me, living in Jerusalem had become like the Arabian Nights. Every woman I met had a story, and every story was an education. I wanted to stay in school.

The dig, for a layman like myself, turned out to be a bust. A grid had been set out over the site with steel rods. Layer after layer of soil had been painstakingly removed to reveal – what? A few crumbling walls, and something Avital told me was once a hearth. I tried to conceal my disappointment. I didn't want to act like an ignoramus, but I guess I tend to do better with what is here, rather than with what you have to imagine out of the past.

Avital led me past a few small trenches, left over from the trial digging, toward a deep pit. 'The pottery!' she proclaimed with genuine enthusiasm. We descended a wooden ladder and joined a huddle of people carrying pointing trowels, shovels, and buckets. When Avital arrived she gave some directions in Hebrew and the helpers dispersed to begin their careful scraping of the layers of the past.

'Well!' I said. 'Some place! Remarkable! Truly remarkable.'

'We've found more than four thousand fragments here,' Avital announced.

'That's impressive,' I replied. '*Four* thousand.' As soon as I spoke I knew that I had put the emphasis on the wrong word. But Avital's first language wasn't English, so perhaps she didn't notice.

I hadn't forgotten about Schoom. In fact, I found myself casing the place, like the burglar he wanted me to be. Now that I was here, stealing something really didn't seem such a big deal. What was one shard give or take four thousand? Let the old guy have his pleasures. He had to listen to me going on about my extraordinary conquests day in and day out. That must have been a trial. True, my sex life was getting me into all kinds of trouble. But the fact remained that I was young and he was old. I was fucking frequently and he, by the looks of him, was in deep misery. If he wanted to caress a two-thousand-year-old pot – then let him.

Am I saying I stole because I felt sorry for Schoom? Maybe. But there was something else: the girl from the waiting room. I had this weird fantasy that bringing home the Schoom-shard would give me a conversation opener with the gorgeous patient who preceded me. 'Hey – I stole for him,' or 'Excuse me a moment but I wonder if we could have coffee after my session. There's something urgent I need to discuss with you about Dr Schoom.' Whatever the reasons, as we were about to make our way out of the pottery I knelt down, ostensibly to tie my sneaker. Avital was halfway up the ladder. I had chosen to stop close to a worker who had collected several fragments on a tray next to him. As he concentrated on his scraping, I stretched out my hand and covered the largest piece of pottery I could see. I stood up and in one smooth gesture pocketed the prize. I walked around slowly until my heart had returned to normal speed, then I headed toward the ladder. When I reached the top, Avital was nowhere to be seen.

One of the archaeologists had noticed her talking with the head of the dig, Avram Fleischer. A telephonist at the site office thought that she had glimpsed her running past the window. The guard in the parking lot told me that he had seen her getting into her car. She had shouted, 'Tell him I couldn't wait any more.'

'Was it an emergency?' I asked, somewhat baffled.

'Maybe,' he said. 'She seemed in a huge hurry.'

There was nothing for it but to make my own way back to Jerusalem. It was Friday. The workers from the dig were all leaving early to get home before the Sabbath. I picked up a ride to a bus stop on the highway. A blur of traffic was speeding in both directions but there was no sign of a bus. I stood in the shade of a eucalyptus tree and took the shard out of my pocket. It hadn't been properly cleaned yet. It looked like, well, a bit of a pot. Maybe, I thought, it's a part of one of those lamps Avital was talking about. Two thousand years ago someone made a little halo of light around himself with what I was holding. And what did he see? The body of the woman beside him. Yes, it was a bedside lamp. I was convinced.

By the time I got to Jerusalem it was dusk. I called Avital from the Egged station but there was no answer. I began to walk home. Then, suddenly, I changed direction. I would drop off the booty at Schoom's place. It was best to get rid of the evidence before catching up with Avital.

The road to Schoom's took me through the orthodox neighbourhood of Me'a She'arim. Its narrow streets were clogged with Hasidim on their way to prayers. Buzzing blackflies. I made my way through courtyards flickering with candlelight, past empty yeshivas, shuttered store-fronts, kerchiefed mothers dragging their last recalcitrant children from cobblestone to hearth. At some point I lost my way and found myself in a cul-de-sac. Two poorly inscribed signs had been hammered above a wooden doorway. The top one gave the name Yeshiva Tarfon; the second read, 'You are not required to complete the task, yet you are not free to withdraw from it.' Was this profound? I wasn't sure.

On Ha'bashim Street, I paused outside Schoom's gate. There was a sweet, almost sickly scent of honeysuckle in the air. The street was deserted. The pink dome of the Ethiopian church loomed over Schoom's little house, like a nipple above the obsessions of his patients. I descended the concrete steps at the far end of the analyst's flower-filled yard, and entered the waiting room.

Schoom, of course, was not a religious man. He held sessions until late in the day on Fridays. When I arrived someone was in his office. Again, my absent-minded shrink, my *sleepy* shrink, had failed to close his door properly. Again, I heard voices. Schoom was talking, very directly. It must have been the end of the session, that point when, after all the silences and sighs, Schoom would finally, almost reluctantly, summarize some of *his* thoughts. 'You cannot possibly go,' he was saying. 'You have already told me that you believe this is not something your mother would have wished you to do. I understand that you do not want to be controlled from beyond the grave. But there are other considerations. Do you think that I will be here when you return? I assure you that it is most unlikely.'

(Ah yes, I thought, the old 'interrupt-the-therapy-and-you'll-never-get-back-on-track' routine.)

'And this man,' Schoom continued, 'this Yacki. Do you really believe that you will lead a productive life in San Diego with a jeweller-hippie? You, who spent four years at the Rubin Academy of Music. And what did your dream tell you? Your frightening dream that you have just recounted. According to your own words, it meant that someone was about to make a terrible mistake.'

There was silence. Someone, patient or analyst, about to make a terrible mistake or not, shifted in their chair. I sat in the advancing purple darkness of Schoom's waiting room. Then she emerged, and, braver than any patient that I had ever imagined, she turned and yelled through the door, 'I can't bear it any more. I want to be free.' In a blur of black mini-skirt and black T-shirt she was gone.

I knocked lightly and put my head around the door. Schoom was seated in shadow behind his desk, his face in his hands. I entered the room tentatively. 'Dr Schoom.' He looked up but did not appear to register my presence. 'I brought you what you wanted.'

Schoom gave me a long look. When I finally came into focus he seemed to make a sudden decision. 'You,' he said (just as my cousin Ruthie had said it). 'Of course. Go after her. You, who claim to know so much about women. Go after her. Tell her, please, what a fool she is being. Go. Go!'

'But I have your antiquity.' I began to search around in my pockets.

'Never mind. I can't listen to you now. Do as I say, please, Go after her.'

I went. I sprinted down Ha'bashim Street, lifting my knees high toward my chest, as I had been taught to do in high school. I pumped my arms and puffed like a steam train. But to where? I chose the un-orthodox direction, Jaffa Road. And yes, there she was, not too far off, turning down an alleyway next to a falafel and schwarma stand where the bright pink torso of a lamb was turning on a spit. I ran, dodging in and out of late shoppers on their way home loaded down with vegetables and bunches of flowers. Schoom had ordered me to the chase. He had authorized my desires. What luck!

I caught up with her outside a shoe store called Sandal-aria where she had stopped to check out the window display. 'Excuse me,' I said, catching my breath. 'I've come from Dr Schoom. He sent me. I mean, I wanted to come anyway. But he asked me. In any case I was going to ask you.'

'What do you want? Who are you?' Her voice was full of irritation, but no surprise – she had been hit on before.

I couldn't very well, at this point, tell her not to go to San Diego with Yacki (what was all that about anyway? The crack in the door had opened into a wide fissure of broken confidentiality), so I said, 'It's a long story and it concerns Dr Schoom. I wonder if we could sit somewhere for a while?'

'You're one of Hillel's patients, aren't you?' she replied. 'I've seen you in the waiting room.'

'Yes,' I said, pleased to acknowledge that we had therapy in common, but disturbed at the same time by her easy use of Schoom's first name. With me it was always *Mr* Winaker and *Dr* Schoom.

We walked up the street and sat in the Ta'amon Café between two tables occupied by chess players. The place was closing. The wizened old waitress was bustling around looking like she didn't want to take another order. I felt pressured and I didn't quite know where to begin. Every time I looked into those green eyes I got unhinged. I mumbled some stuff about being an economist (she looked bored), mouthed a few platitudes about Israel, and then plucked out of the air, 'How long have you been in therapy with Dr Schoom?'

She started to laugh. 'Therapy?' she replied. 'All my life. He's my father.'

Okay, okay. If you're thinking I was turned on by this information, you're right. I experienced a brief moment of decline, a perceptible sliding down on the parabola of my desire when the incest taboo first kicked in, but this was quickly reversed. Schoom's daughter! The possibilities (the incestuous possibilities) were endless. There was also a feeling of larceny. He had made me steal, and in doing so he had stolen something from me. Now, I would take from him.

So I launched into my seductive rap – and I could be quite charming. ('You turn your aggression into charm." – Dr Hillel Schoom) After all, seduction was almost an occupation with me and I worked hard at it. 'What are you on?' Avital had asked in one of our bitter moments. 'A sexual crusade?'

Aviva (that was her name) heard me out while I name-dropped, sprinkled a couple of witticisms, and described my must-see Jerusalem apartment ('set in a walled garden, the scent of oleanders, olive tree overhanging the balcony, once owned by an artist, eccentric landlady former mistress of Moshe Dayan, stars beautiful from the *mirpesset*, blah blah blah'), then she paused, just like her father, before speaking. 'Look,' she said. 'You seem like an intelligent man, but I can tell you right now that I'm not attracted to you sexually.'

The waitress had appeared at my shoulder. 'Bruised ego, please,' I said, 'and could you put a little crushed testicle into the coffee?'

'Same for you sweetheart?' she asked Aviva. Aviva declined.

My drink and cheque arrived simultaneously. I realized that, in the general sense of rush, I had failed to do Schoom's bidding. Aviva must be wondering why her father had sent me after her. But what could I say – 'Don't go to San Diego with Yacki. Come home with me instead?' It was ridiculous.

'Listen,' Aviva was saying. 'I really have to go. So if you could give me my father's message.' I loved her rolled r's and singsong Israeli accent, so different from her father's Euro-snob sibilated utterances.

I stared at her. Around her neck she wore a bright cobalt blue enamelled Star of David, no doubt one of Yacki's creations. 'Your father,' I stuttered, 'wanted me' (long pause) 'to give you this!' Triumphantly, I produced the shard from my pocket. Then I improvised: 'He didn't have time to take it. He was preoccupied with an emergency – a phone call. He asked me to give it to you. He wants you to hold it for him, then return it to him. As soon as possible.' She took the piece of pottery in her hand, stood up and dropped it in her leather bag. 'Okay,' she said. 'No problem.'

'Any chance we could go out one night this week?' I begged pathetically.

'How old are you?' she asked.

'Thirty-eight.'

'You need to be younger.'

I smiled virtuously, as if I would make every effort to do as she wished. Then I put my hand to my head and looked down despairingly. Her tanned legs, strapped up calf-high with the long lavender ribbons of her espadrilles, disappeared through the café door.

When I got home there was a message on my answering machine. It was Avital. She spoke in a trembling voice that said, 'If you do not return what you stole I will report you to the police.' Shame and disgrace! I dialled her number in a panic. I had no idea what I would say to her. How had she found out anyway? Some shifty-eyed digger must have seen me. I let the phone ring ten, twenty times. No answer. I was sweating so much my feet felt as if they were swimming in my sandals. There was nothing for it but to return to Schoom's. But I had to take a shower first. I stood under the weak drizzle that was the best I could ever get in Jerusalem, and tried to scrub away my guilt. Dressing, I chose a white shirt and cream-coloured pants. How could a person as clean as me go to jail?

I left my apartment and ran around the back of the Hamashbir department store to Ben Yehuda Street. The cafés had all pulled in their tables and chairs; the centre of town was deserted. There was this overwhelming Sabbath atmosphere that gets me every time, even though I am a person who believes we are lucky there is no God. Anyway, the atmosphere, whatever it was – a violet-stained tranquil path, dust and blessings – slowed me to a walk. I crossed Zion Square and headed up the hill to Schoom's street. I felt momentarily pulled up from my troubles. As usual, this elevation was accomplished by the surface of things: the pink stone of the houses under starlight, the scent of jasmine, the distant cry of the muezzin – all the heady stuff that the city had to offer. But what lay under the sights, smells, and sounds? Something about the place that I didn't want to know? Something about myself?

Schoom's office was locked, so I had to go to the front of the house. I noticed immediately a brightly coloured, oversized mezuzah on the portal of his door. 'Former owners,' I thought, but no, a matching ceramic nameplate – DR HILLEL SCHOOM, entwined with painted flowers – had been nailed above the knocker.

Schoom came to the door. His shirt was uncharacteristically open, there were patches of sweat under his arms, and his face looked drawn and tired. 'Well,' he said, 'did you convince her?'

I wanted to say, 'You're out of your mind,' but it seemed unnecessary. I think he knew. I let him lead me into his sitting room – leather chairs, kilims, subtle abstracts on the walls (originals by local artists). Shrinks, I thought, always tasteful. It was part of the whole quiet, restrained, unobtrusive thing.

Schoom looked like he might shake me if I didn't speak, so I said, 'I'm in bigger trouble than your daughter.' I told him the story. I expected him to take the blame, or at least part of the blame, and then walk over to the phone and call Aviva. Instead, he gave a short, sharp, unhappy laugh.

'Well,' he said, 'now, at last, you have a real problem.'

'What's that supposed to mean?'

'Oh,' he waved his hand at me, 'surely you must be aware of your own silliness. This business with women. Your ceaseless talk about this one and that one. Your ridiculous daily conquests. You are obsessed with the

quotidian. Do you know that in your year-and-a-half of
therapy you have not once taken the opportunity to present me with a dream?'

'That's not true. What about the hallah that fought my
father's prayer shawl, and had the number seven cut into
one of its braids?'

Schoom looked at me with contempt. How, I wondered,
could he disdain a dream? I thought they were value-free.
'You want to alter your behaviour,' Schoom continued,
'or at least you say you do. But you can't change the
present without coming to terms with the past. I have
tried, you know, to direct you back, but you resist. All
you want to do is tell me stories about bed. I *know* the
bed.'

'What about when my father collapsed? You fell asleep.'

'Nonsense, nonsense. I was waiting for the memory to
lead you somewhere, to a *reflection*. But no, your father
collapses in your memory and you can go no further. The
next minute you are again plotting a seduction. Perhaps
there is a connection between the two thoughts, but how
could you possibly find it? Every time you have a piece
of the past in your hands you throw it away.'

It was a piece of the past that had got me into all this
trouble. But what was the use of arguing with Schoom?
He had nastily transformed from therapist to antagonist.
And the realization had slowly dawned on me (the 'resistance' was great) that Schoom *didn't like me*.

'Look,' I said, 'I didn't come here to be scolded. I have
to retrieve the shard. Please call your daughter, or else
give me her number or address.'

'My daughter, your saviour, has doubtless already
passed on what you gave her to her feckless boyfriend.
He, the marvellous Yacki, who knows even less than
you about the world he wanders through, is probably
stringing the shard for a pendant at this very moment.'

Oh, give them a break, I thought, a break from all this
knowledge and history. Let them wander in the San Diego

desert and smoke dope. Where was it written that everyone has to be weighed down by the stones of Jerusalem? Let them float on their backs in the Pacific wearing nothing but their pendants and earrings. To hell with the past.

Schoom sat down heavily in one of his swivel armchairs. 'You will not find them,' he said. 'They are leaving tonight for California. This, I see, my daughter did not tell you. They are probably at the airport right now.'

Ben Gurion was forty minutes from Jerusalem. It was never easy to find a taxi on a Friday night. I had no money in my pockets. Schoom had no idea what airline they were using. My situation was hopeless.

Outside, a summer thundershower was sending fat drops of rain onto the dusty sidewalk. A police car followed me down the street (they know already!) and then turned off up a hill toward the Old City. There was nothing for it but to plead with Avital to be merciful. The rain blew in sheets across Jaffa Road staining the low buildings apple-grey. My shirt was soaked through, transparent. I walked to a phone booth, but didn't have a token. I had to call collect. I heard the operator say my name. There was a short wait and then Avital, sounding extremely angry, said, 'Have you got it?'

It had been a long day. There was water dripping off my head onto my glasses. I started to go through the whole thing. I think I began by saying, 'I was sitting outside Schoom's office . . .' but Avital interrupted me.

'What you stole was valuable. It came from the most productive layer of the site. How could you do that? Do you even know what you stole? You took the intact handle of a two-thousand-year-old oil lamp!'

I was about to say, 'I thought it might be something like that,' but being pleased with myself for guessing right was not an appropriate response. 'Well, it's gone,' I said. 'It's on its way to California.' Avital started to speak very fast. I put the phone back on its hook.

Where to go? The rain had eased up a little, but miniature flash floods were rolling through the gutters. Only
one person could get me out of this mess: Schoom. But I
had nothing left to say to him. And he was clearly finished
with me. Nevertheless I found myself returning once
again to Ha'bashim Street, and once again I stood outside
his door. There were no lights at the front of the house
and no one answered when I knocked. I squeezed around
a side alley, scratching my arms on the bushes that overhung Schoom's neighbour's wall. A diffuse, fuzzy light
filled a square of window halfway down the side of the
house. An upturned tin bucket that was lying in the alley
gave me the pedestal I needed. Two candles were burning
on a desk. Otherwise, the room was in darkness. Schoom
was bent low over his work. Carefully, with meticulous,
guarded movements of his hands, Schoom was cleaning
the shard.

Physically Correct

January 12, 1991

I sit in Papa Gino's with my ten-year-old son. In front of
him is a slice of pepperoni, an 'adult-sized' ziti, and a
medium Coke. He wants to talk about Adam and Eve.
'How did Adam know what it was like to be a child?' he
asks me. In the background the Beach Boys sing about a
Caribbean island, and the girl they want to take there. A
woman in a Papa Gino's Special Thursday Night Chef's
hat wipes down the table next to us. Four office workers
squeeze by her. Into my silence my son injects an answer.
'He must have had to have asked his kids.'

Nothing is going well for me these days. I am losing
my job, and my heart has an inverted T-wave and a
murmur. Dr Seagrave has ordered me to take a stress test
at the end of the month. I will put on sneakers and walk
and run for miles, if I last, on a treadmill. Meanwhile the
college's insurance company has turned me down for
long-term disability. They do not like the look of my
electro-cardiogram.

'How could Adam and Eve have a baby if they weren't
married?' This is easier, especially as we have been over
the topic before. I conclude my explanation with an offer.

'You remember that book about having a baby that your
cousin Ben sent you (desperate to get it out of his own
house), the one with the pictures and the diagrams? We
could read it when we get home.'

'No thanks,' says Dan. 'I've already seen all that at
school, with the ear.'

I know immediately what he means. Diagrams. The
inner ear. Tubes, caves, crevices. Enough with internal

organs. Let them be. Last week I saw my own heart on an echo-cardiogram, the valves opening and closing, the great systole and diastole of life made visible. I saw a wind instrument. The technician, bending to observe the screen, caught a murmur, but no music.

My job. How shall I say it? I have been accused. Things have been alleged, insinuations made, the air is thick with innuendo. I am the Beast of Malden. A student (ah, readers, you think you know what is coming) has paid a visit to the chairperson of my department. She feels, apparently, that during 'Planets and Stars' (Astronomy 131) I 'eroticized her with looks'. She wanted, she told the chair, to 'register her feeling of discomfort'. Overnight I became Humbert Humbert, Don Giovanni, a telephone sex-line caller.

It is possible that I looked. There are two hundred students in the class. Everyone wants to know about planets and stars. We gaze into the universe. It looks like a big nothing with a handful of glitter. The gaze returns to earth. Sometimes I look around the class. I'm sure I looked.

Flesh and blood. Rice cakes and seltzer water. If only I were made of the latter, like Professor Norma Szec who has picked up the campaign against me. My informers tell me that Professor Szec is offended by my 'libidinous heterosexuality'. They have let me know that she will stop at nothing to root me out of the department. How could I, she wants to know, acting *in loco parentis*, have dared to look?

It is true that no one, not even myself, knows what I saw. Could it have been *cleavage*? I remember none. And in December? Unlikely. But then again, perhaps, in the overheated classroom, as a sweater was being pulled off, and before the emerging flushed face in a shirt with two or three buttons undone had been able to concentrate itself?

Maybe? Perhaps? Who knows? God did not offer Moses

his face. But suppose God had appeared as breasts, suppose God *was* breasts. The patriarch, I am betting, even if warned to avert his eyes, would have looked.

Professor Szec has very small breasts. This is a statement of fact, not the manifestation of an obsession. She is a specialist in nebulae, gas, dust in space. I have heard her lecture eloquently on what is, after all, next to nothing. She also teaches our 'Women and Astronomy' course, and is the author of a book on Henrietta Leavitt (1862–1921) the great American astro-physicist who discovered that Cepheid variables could be used for distance finding. Thanks to Henrietta we know that our nearest galaxy, Andromeda, is two million light years away.

Professor Szec and I do not communicate. I see her red hair disappearing around corners. She sees my eyes fix on the wall behind her. Letitia Birnbaum, the source of all my distress, is in Paris for the semester. Her meeting with the chairperson took place shortly before Christmas. He looked her in the eyes (I believe that they are green) and she told him her story. Outside, the chapel bells tolled, and the university chorale sang 'O come, O come Emanuel'. As the story has circulated, the irony of this moment has been lost on no one, for that is my name, Emanuel Levitan, Hoyle Professor of Reckless Eyeballing, and no doubt, in the mind of Professor Szec, Purveyor of Ejaculations to the Stars.

January 30

The furore is effecting my family. My wife has taken to calling me 'Marion', after the unfortunate mayor of Washington DC. She refers to herself as 'Effie', the name of the mayor's wife. Effie, you will remember, stood by her man until the trial was over, and then she left him. I have imagined myself on videotape, a crack pipe on my desk, Letitia Birnbaum pinned to the floor of my office by a sexually ferocious look. She writhes and twists, her fingers play between her legs, with her free hand she rubs her breasts in slow circles. She moans, 'Stop, please, no more,' but *I will not stop looking at her*.

February 2

The failure of the Hubble telescope has left everyone in our department depressed, except for Professor Szec. This semester she is teaching 'Stars and Stripes: Colonized Space and the Phallicized Moon'. I have learned from a mutual student that according to Professor Szec the American telescope should not have been sent up in the first place. We must not look too far into the beyond: it is, analogically, a patriarchal attempt to possess the universal womb, to re-enter, via telescopic images, the unknowable nothing of female interiority.

Earlier today, a strange incident. Professor Spingold's daughter Cynthia, a freshperson at our school, happened to run into her father in the corridors of the Science Building. She lives in the dorms, and, not having seen her father for a while, she hugged and embraced him. Within an hour poor Spingold was on the mat in front of the chairperson. Like me, he had been reported, a student (Melinda Chabanian) had witnessed his behaviour, and, taking Spingold's daughter for a young student lover, and the professor's public behaviour to be unseemly, she decided on the spot to inform.

Naturally, as soon as Spingold was able to speak, our chairman became embarrassed and apologized profusely. He did not, however, altogether back off. 'You must,' he told Spingold, 'try to avoid even the appearance of impropriety.' Spingold told me this story as we stood by the coffee machine. As he finished, Professor Szec walked by with an attractive female colleague from Community Health. They both wore startling, and obviously expensive, outfits. Spingold and I lowered our eyes.

February 17

Professor Szec believes that I should join a twelve step programme. This has been reported to me by a mutual colleague. It is not clear what I need to cure myself of. I do drink the occasional glass of wine or beer. I even get high sometimes, but I am light years away from addiction. Are there twelve steps to renewed sensitivity? Perhaps a pair of heavily lacquered mirror sunglasses would do the job. But I must not be glib.

Sadly, Professor Szec is having trouble in her own marriage. Her husband is a gambler, a high roller whom the casinos fly down to Atlantic City at their own expense. When he is there, he drinks and plays the crap tables, perhaps he also has affairs. He has a large private income and can afford to lose enormous sums of money before it hurts. On rare occasions, however, he has gone too far. In the old days, when we were friendly colleagues, I once found Professor Szec crouched down in tears behind the photocopying machine. 'Jeremy's blown it,' she said, 'we've had to sell the Datsun.' The machine was spitting out copies of her handout for the day ('Astronut Lunacy: Planting the Flagpole in the Reluctant Crater'). I comforted her as best I could. For ten years she has been trying to wean him away from the crap tables. He will not budge.

February 26

Snow. The sky is milky white and the stars are obscured.

March 1

Professor Shinkin, who is old, and whose work on gravity waves has led his name to be whispered in conjunction with that magic constellation of letters, 'Nobel Prize', is in trouble. Unable at seventy (he is to retire at the end of this year) to accommodate the sudden shifts in nomenclature engendered by our current crisis, he continues to pronounce the remote planet between Saturn and Neptune as 'Your Anus'. In class the other day, speculating that the Earth may be no more than the residue of a massive primordial cloud, Professor Shinkin got side-tracked into a discussion of Voyager II. Shinkin announced to the students that years ago he had begun to hope that Voyager would 'uncover the moons of Uranus'. There was a brief disturbance, some books were knocked to the ground and several young men and women exited. The radical caucus made straight for the sympathetic ear of Professor Szec. Hastily deconstructed, Shinkin's wistful phrase emerged in bio-political terms as an assault on a large buttocked girl who always sits alone in the front row, squeezed awkwardly into the too-small space that the chair designer thoughtlessly provided. Prof. Shinkin ('Kinky-Shinky' as one of the students described him to general but speedily controlled laughter in Professor Szec's office – this was a serious matter), it was claimed, could not take his eyes off the protruding orbs. The students had come to Norma to protest on the girl's behalf. True, the lookee remained in class, oblivious to both insult and violation, but those who cannot stand up for themselves must be defended by the strong. Professor Szec bravely took on the case.

Today, we have all received a memo from our chairperson. He reminds us that we must at all times take care to say 'Urinous'. What a sour-smelling stream the new pronunciation conjures. But if I am to keep my job I must watch my tongue.

March 15

A conversation with Shinkin over lunch. He believes that one day in the not-too-distant future one of the large but delicate instruments constructed on our campus will identify and measure a gravity wave. In time we may pick up a ripple from the Big Bang itself. Turning our telescope to the area the wave comes in on, we will be able to witness the beginning of our universe. We will gaze into the night sky and discover our own birth. I am a scientist and should not be troubled by this astonishing possibility. And yet, I ask myself: Are there some things from which we should avert our eyes? Cameras in the delivery rooms. Perhaps we should stop.

March 21

Down to Room 69 for our faculty mandated sensitivity-raising session. Professor Iliopoulos, a shy man in his late sixties, admitted that he had last week referred to one of the waitresses in the faculty dining room as 'my dear girl'. He apologized in our meeting and was forgiven by Norma Szec. Elspeth Bose-Einstein, the youngest member of our department, had a strange tale to tell. It seems that, during a lecture on administrative procedures for new faculty, she was grabbed and bitten on the arm by a high-ranking dean. The bite was apparently intended as a metaphoric representation of potential parental ferocity in the face of a favourite child's bad grades. ('They pay twenty thousand a year, downgrade their kids and you will get hurt.') My reaction to this strange tale was to think, 'This dean is demented.' Bose-Einstein, though, had another interpretation for his behaviour: she had been humiliated and taken advantage of *simply because she did not have tenure*. She was weak, the dean strong; hence she could be bitten with impunity. To my astonishment, there was general concurrence that the biting was indeed an act not of madness but discrimination.

March 26

My cholesterol, the bad type, is up to 293 but I am still stuffing myself with hamburgers. I cannot help it. In two days my case comes before the preliminary board. Letitia Birnbaum has written a letter from Paris documenting her side of the story. Thus far, I have not been permitted to see a copy. This morning, as I was leaving for work, my son asked me, 'Do they come to shovel the snow off graves?'

March 28

The Chairman of the Committee is sick with flu and I have been granted a week's reprieve. Last night, unable to sleep, I read the Book of Job. I was particularly struck by God's question/reprimand: 'Where wast thou when I laid the foundations of the earth? Declare, if thou hast understanding. Who hath laid the measures thereof, if thou knowest? Or who hath stretched the line upon it? Whereupon are the foundations thereof fastened? Or who laid the cornerstone thereof; when the morning stars sang together and all the sons of God shouted for joy?' The question, of course, is not where was Job, but where was God? If Shinkin is right we may soon know. Finally asleep, I dreamed myself at work in an office with a glass door. A small crowd of my colleagues had gathered to look through from the outside. Between their thighs they held inverted telescopes that rapidly collapsed and elongated. Letitia Birnbaum, wearing nothing but an enormous pair of yellow-rimmed glasses (the kind that children sometimes purchase at street fairs), was peppering me with questions: 'Was there a singular event at the beginning? Did we unfurl in a sea of unknowable desire? Was the universe once dense, hot and small?' I woke in a sweat, repeating her words, 'dense, hot and small', groaning.

'More bad dreams, Marion?' asked my wife.

'Enough,' I begged. 'Enough.'

April 1

A cold icy rain all morning. I sit in my office for the longest time, staring straight ahead while the sleet taps on the window. On my desk, a copy, forwarded by the Dean, of Letitia Birnbaum's letter from Paris. Her Junior Year Abroad is not helping her English. Her letter also reveals a bias towards illustration. Wherever there are 'o's present, as in the word 'look', Letitia has drawn two dots to transform the letters into cartoon eyes. Are breasts to be inferred as well? Only a beast like myself would think so.

'Dear Profs,' the document begins, 'Norma' (crossed out) 'Prof. Szec told me that it would be a good idea if I put down on paper what happened with me and Prof. Levitan. Well, he was talking about something and to tell the truth I wasn't really listening coz I was reading *The Groundhog* which although it is a student newspaper does print Calvin and Hobbes which I like. Anyway, Michael Struzziery who always sits next to me in the lectures (although we are not going out) nudged me and said that perhaps I'd better pay attention coz Levitan was going to talk about the exam. When it was going to be and how long. I started laughing. I don't know why and Prof. Levitan looked at me as if to say, you know, "Can you be quiet please?" or something, coz he'd lost his train of thought. He had this big diagram on the board behind him. So I bit my tongue and looked at Michael's notes and I saw that he'd written "The universe is expanding" and then something about hydrogen and helium. This part is really my fault because I started thinking about a time when some friends at a party had swallowed helium out of a tank we'd brought along for balloons and then they (not me in case you were thinking that) had all started talking in high-pitched voices and it was *so* funny. So I started giggling again and Prof. Levitan gave me this really dirty look. And I think he had every right too' (dotted 'o's) 'then because I was kind of interrupting the class although I didn't mean to. But the point anyway is that after I stopped laughing he just kind of kept on staring at me every time he looked up from his notes. Now I am pretty attractive even if I have to say so myself and Norma' (crossed out) 'Prof. Szec thinks that it is important to say so in some way where you will know I am a self-aware person. I get hit on by a lot of guys some of whom are quite cool and *I know* when someone is coming on to me. So Levitan, Prof. Levitan that is, who is actually not a bad looking guy and quite intelligent although he does tend to sweat a lot and when his hair gets matted down on his head he looks really icky, he, it seemed to me was looking at me in *that kind of way* if you know what I mean. And then Michael Struzziery leaned over my notepad and did this real funny drawing of Levitan with a bubble coming out of his mouth saying "I want you baaaaaad". And I thought, well, I'm not *crazy* then.' The letter closed with the words *A Bientôt*, a florid extravagant signature, and a P.S. etched in hand-printed capitals: 'HE LOOKED AT ME AND I WAS UNCOMFORTABLE. NORMA DID NOT TELL ME TO SAY THIS.'

April 2

Return to Papa Gino's for the Fourth Grade soccer team's Thursday Night Pizza Party. I am Assistant Coach. Tonight we are all in a good mood after a smashing defeat of the Waban Caribou – except my son. He sits off to one side, slouched in the corner of a booth, while his friends whoop it up. When I ask what is the matter, he replies, 'I'm thinking, leave me alone.'

When I go to pick up the pizza I overhear two employees discussing the recent gall-bladder surgery of one of them. 'Do you know what is the worst part?' asks a balding, middle-aged man, who, in his hunched demeanour, reminds me of myself. 'The first shit afterwards.' He turns to me, and asks, 'Seventy-Two? Three large half extra-cheese half pepperoni? Nine cokes?'

Back at the tables already covered with swirling patterns of salt, pepper and parmesan cheese, Daniel seems to have come around. 'What was bothering you?' I ask, as he grabs a slice, bites, and begins to negotiate the rubbery-looking cheese.

'Oh, nothing,' he replies, 'just a dream I had.'

'Was it a scary dream?'

'Not really. I dreamed that God and I were young together and we did not know what death was.'

My son is ten years old, he loves baseball and TV. In the mornings he goes happily to school to study primitive algebra and current events, he takes spelling tests, observes the development of tadpole to frog. He teases others and is teased. As far as I know, religion and cosmology are not part of his curriculum.

Leaving the restaurant the stars were spread across the sky like tumbled jewels on velvet. They are fires, of course, gases, minerals, heat, atoms. And beyond, where God is young, in the empty playroom, where no one is looking, he piles nothing on nothing until it all comes crashing down.

April 3

Whispers and conspiracy. Professor Szec has agglomerated. I have learned from Maggie, the Vice Chancellor's secretary and my neighbour's sister, that two professors from outside the department have rolled into Szec's ball. Sidney Mendrick (Ancient History) and our campus's Bright Young Thing, Brian Rotweiler (International Relations), a prizewinner and frequent talking head on our local TV stations, have co-penned a letter to the highest authorities. They have written *sub rosa*, I surmise, because the three of us share some influential acquaintances. My colleagues do not want word of their pusillanimity to get out. According to Maggie, their letter expresses concern. They have been made aware of Letitia's charges. They feel, as old *friends* of mine, betrayed by my behaviour. Somehow I must be censored, blinkered, made to understand that I cannot look without thinking first. Perhaps the VC can encourage me to resign?

Looks! Mendrick paces, staring at the ground. He patrols the corridors of our university, muttering and grousing. Undertone, intrigue and concealment are his

stimulants. It is clear my case excites him. As for Rotweiler, the only looks he gives are over the shoulder.
His search for the faces of the powerful and famous is
unending. Beyond the rarefied air of our university town,
where name-drops are more frequent than rain, he would
choke and die. Friends! I taste the salt on my lips.

April 5

Torrential rain. I attend a late-afternoon lecture on gamma
ray bursts. In the car park, under the sharp thrills of
lightning and the rumble of thunder, I find that my car
will not start. The plugs are wet and even as I try to dry
them they soak again. I decide to walk home. My route
takes me through a small park. I squelch through puddles;
water soaks through my socks and into my shoes. The
rain pours on my bare head, mists up my glasses, and
quilts dark patches into my coat. To be drenched, I decide,
is not unpleasant. Under a lamp post I suddenly realize
that I have (by chance?) arrived outside Norma Szec's
front gate. A lone dogwood sapling, squarely situated in
the middle of her lawn, its thin branches lifting this way
and that in the wind, is trying to break into bud. I am
overtaken with confusion. To enter or not to enter?

I approach the narrow ground-floor windows of the old
Victorian town house. I stand on tip toes in the flower
border, trying to avoid the fresh sprung crocus and snow-
drop shoots. I peer through thin lace curtains, to where,
in the funnelled light from a TV screen, Norma Szec and
a student I recognize from 'Planets and Stars' sit in still-
ness and silence. The boy, Arno Penzias, an extremely
intelligent young man, wears nothing but his under-
shorts. Professor Szec, rigid in a white slip, her body
shaped to her hard-backed chair in precise right angles,
stares at the screen, while her left hand, disappeared into
the dark matter of Penzias's briefs, moves slowly, almost
tediously, up and down.

The most beautiful experience we can have, Einstein

tells us, is the mysterious. 'Whosoever does not know it and can no longer wonder, no longer marvel, is as good as dead, and his eyes are dimmed.' Dear Norma and Penzias, we look to penetrate the mysteries. When we have gone as far as we can go we scribble 'Here be dragons' in the margins, like the old cartographers. Keep on at your handpump! The laws of motion, the sweet Newtonian concept of acceleration will take you the distance.

April 9

The day of the hearing. I eat breakfast, a large bowl of mini Shredded Wheats with blueberry centres, zero fat, zero cholesterol, while my wife scans the paper. She announces a sale of lingerie at Filene's Basement; perhaps I might want to drop by on my way to the hearing. I could, she suggests, pick up a little something. Perhaps one of my favourite students will drop by my office later in the day. Outside, the children squabble over who will sit in the front of the car. When I drop them off Daniel says, 'Kick butt, Dad.' He has no messages from God.

The department lounge, its walls strung with mounted photographs of earth as seen from space (strange, for our profession tends to look the other way), has been converted into a mini-courtroom. Two long tables have been pushed together and a black cloth stretched over them. Seated at the table are our chairperson, Victor Broglie; three members of the Physics department (our mother ship); Deirdre Occam, the university's troubleshooting Dean of Undergraduate Studies; and Norman Braithwaite from Theology.

As the evidence against me mounts, I find myself distracted. I hear the false notes of Letitia Birnbaum's letter as it is read aloud, the derisive jabs of Norma Szec's 'undressed with his eyes', 'assault', 'invasion', and (do I dream this?) 'ravishing'. But it is all background music. I am entirely caught up in the symbolic interchange of looks that my hearing has occasioned. I note that Chippy Wigner from Physics is most definitely fixed on the bursting buttons of Deirdre Occam's blouse. Similarly, Professor Betsy Perlman is staring into the eyes of Victor Broglie with what appears to be unmuted passion. Everyone, in an orgy of visual desire, is looking at everyone else. Yes! We must remember our creatureliness. Truly, we looked before we spoke, knew desire before we spoke, danced before we spoke, perhaps even loved before we spoke.

Broglie calls me to attention. Professor Szec is detailing the decline in teaching standards in Physics/Astronomy departments all over the country. She cites a story from one of our most prestigious institutions. A professor who should have known better (he was close to retirement age) thought to absorb his students in the subtle differentiations of waves and oscillations by bringing a belly-dancer into the classroom. He was suspended for the remainder of the semester and obliged to write a public letter of apology to the female and male-feminist students whom he had offended. Personally, Professor Szec thought the suspension a little harsh; after all, the professor's crime was stupidity, not the more dangerous personal invasiveness with which I was charged.

When the time came for me to speak, the room was already spinning. The black cloth from the table soared, first like a kite, then like a billowing tent, above my head. In this firmament orbited the pale faces of my judges and accusers, spherical planets in the crystalline heavens. In my vertigo, heart pumping, I sensed the end. The burgers, pizza and Coco-Puffs I had finished from my kids' breakfast bowls, surfed, arms outstretched, on the summits and declines of my inverted T-waves. My cholesterol came up to meet me, a big three followed by a surging crowd of zeroes.

The next thing I knew I was in the arms of Norman Braithwaite, my head resting on his knee, Victor Broglie, surrounded, it seemed to me, by a pure blue ray, was waving a Chap-Stick (why?) under my nose. To my shame, they all seemed to know that what I had suffered was not a heart attack, but a blackout.

April 11

Victory! Norma's epigones had a Freudian field day with my fainting fit. But too late, too late! Letitia Birnbaum has withdrawn the charges. A letter arrived from Pamplona. Letitia has absconded from her semester at the Sorbonne. She has also traded mentors. In place of Norma is a young Spanish entrepreneur in the compact disc business. Javier, as she frequently refers to him in her letter, is teaching her a lot. They lie naked in bed, and if Letitia is to be believed, they do not touch. Javier plans to 'spend a three month transition period' staring into Letitia's eyes. True, at the time of writing he has only gone three days, and this while Letitia recovers from a stomach virus contracted after eating a seafood *paella*, but Javier holds the eyes to be deep wells of wisdom. Our student is also coming to terms with her own irresistibility and what she now calls her 'erotic makeup'. She is willing to concede, in retrospect, and from the vantage point that Javier has taught her, that what she felt in 'Planets and Stars' may have arisen from within. One sour note. When I tell my wife that I am exonerated she replies, 'Well, Marion, I guess you beat the rap.'

April 15

In my kitchen, over a lettuce-and-tomato sandwich, Daniel explains the dynamics of his fourth-grade class. He takes two long, thin wooden strips from his brother's Magnet Face Kit and attaches them to the fridge. 'This is the boys' he says, 'and this is the girls.' He pauses. 'Anybody ever tell you about parallel lines, Dad?'

We read the stars as promises of the future, but their light set out many years ago, and the places from which it emanated are at peace. Outside, turning towards the darkening sky, looking for news, I feel with absolute certainty that I am observed. Although I know with equal assurance that my gaze will not be returned.

Omaha

The steam train that passed through the park behind our house, shunting freight to Cricklewood Junction, had come and gone. A pillar of white smoke lay folded over the bare planes and oaks. I was staring out of the window, waiting, as always in those nights, for an air-raid siren to send me scuttling towards the cupboard under the stairs. Suddenly my father burst in, grabbed me from behind, and, bellowing in a deep voice I had never heard before, pulled me with enormous force towards my bedroom door. My mother appeared behind him in her nightgown, screaming 'Lew! Lew!' and began tugging at his shirt. But his strength was superhuman. In a moment he had us both down the stairs and, encircling us with one strong arm so that we wouldn't escape back into the house, he had thrust open the front door and pushed us out into the frigid night air. In the strange, sexual baritone that had taken him over, my father shouted 'Fire! Fire!' into our blacked-out street.

Our neighbour, Mrs Salter, who was used to alarms by now, this being the second year of the Luftwaffe's blitz on London, reacted by scurrying out of her house and towards the shelter her husband had constructed at the foot of their garden. However, as soon as her slippered feet touched the frosted grass of the lawn, she awoke to the fact that she had heard no siren, and that no one could see what my father was seeing.

When the fire in my father's head subsided, he lapsed into silence. Shortly, as we stood shivering under cold stars, a policeman came and laid a heavy hand on his arm. Still later, our family doctor, who had a gentler touch, turned up. My father sat in our kitchen, stonefaced and absent. I heard an ambulance pull up, and then he was gone.

My mother and I must have needed symbolic fortification that night, for, after the hospital had called to say that my father had been admitted, we walked quickly over the road and, although there was no air raid, we spent the night in our neighbours' shelter.

The Salters' Anderson shelter was not much safer than our own cupboard, but its corrugated iron roof and sandbagged entrance gave the impression of stalwart resistance. It was the place to which we repaired during the worst nights of the Blitz, when the skies over the park were criss-crossed with wide, eerie searchlight beams, ack-ack guns boomed, and the rows of Nissen huts housing our local gunners glowed hellishly in the red light of nearby explosions. So it was no accident that the Salters' shelter was also the place in which we chose to survive this latest blow.

After a night of fitful sleep, we went to visit my father. He sat mute and immobile in a worn leather armchair in the corner of a large room. The windows of his ward had been blacked out during the night, and it seemed that in daylight no one was bothering to remove the screens. My father wore broad striped pyjamas under a brown dressing gown with frayed lapels. My mother talked to him while I sat and tried to distract myself from crying by thinking about football scores. My father's silence was somehow animated. He had a look on his face that communicated, above all, shame and embarrassment. When he shifted his head to look around the room, he avoided my eyes.

My father was known in our neighbourhood as a consummate gentleman. To the Jews on our street, many of whom were refugees from Hitler's Europe, he appeared highly anglicized and enviably assimilated. As he was also a well-known figure in synagogue administration, my father was doubly admired. As English gentleman, he tipped his hat to ladies on the street, was rude to no one, and dressed conservatively. As knowledgeable Jew-in-residence, he treated with the utmost attention and seriousness our uneducated 'business' neighbours' requests for advice on how they should conduct their family weddings, bar mitzvahs and *shivahs* in the appropriately Anglo-Jewish way. From this dignified, 'like-us-but-also-like-them' position that my father had earned and occupied without vanity in our community, the fall of a nervous breakdown was long and hard. More than this, as a husband and father whose every action was an offering to the hard God of duty, he must have felt himself a terrible failure to be hospitalized at such a time. Was this why he couldn't look me in the face?

Before leaving, my mother spoke with the doctor. They walked up and down the corridor outside the ward while I sat on a bench and watched them. I strained forward as they came within range and tried to piece together what they were saying from the odd words and phrases that floated my way. Hospitals were not new to me. My father had been in and out of them for as long as I could remember. His heart problems, malfunctioning valves damaged by the rheumatic fever he had suffered as a child, had laid him low on many occasions, and once already had brought him close to death. But this was something new, never before had he lost his mind. The doctor talked about 'Lew's sinations' (I wondered why he called my father by his first name) and 'eye defects'. He talked about my father's medication, and I, who knew all his pills, colour-coded, by heart, heard enough to understand that recovery from his current breakdown would be long, and that the risks to his general health would not at all be diminished by this hospital stay.

As we were about to go I looked through the window of the door to the ward. My father was staring at the floor, his lower lip pushed out; he looked utterly humiliated.

On the way home it was my turn to feel ashamed, for, in truth, I was relieved to leave behind the dreary corridors and strict, stuffy nurses of the Willesden General Hospital. When I asked my mother what was wrong with my father she simply replied, 'Don't worry, he'll be home soon.' Perhaps because I wanted to believe her, but more likely because I already knew the opposite to be true, I let the lie go past.

'But what,' I said, 'about Dad's sinations? And his sight, can he see?'

My mother acted as if she hadn't heard me. When I repeated the questions she replied, 'I don't know what you're talking about. Of course he can see.'

Back home, on our damaged street, my pressing problem was Mr Walsh. Not only had this neighbour of ours refused to return my football after I had deflected it over his fence during an imaginary Cup Final, but he had also insinuated to my mother (this I overheard) that my father's 'heart problems' and subsequent military deferment were not wholly without relation to the fact that he was a Jew. At night I prayed for Walsh's obliteration. I wanted a bomb, like the one that had put a deep crater at the far end of our street, to wipe out the Walsh home, leaving only my football intact.

Walsh did not use the Salters' shelter. There was only accommodation for four, and lately things had become quite cramped through the addition of a fifth person. Until his breakdown, my father had spent his nights firewatching on the roof of the United Synagogue building in Tavistock Square, so he was never with us during the raids. Mr Salter, who had built the shelter, was now in Burma, and, judging by the photographs that he sent back, quite enjoying himself. He wore a dashing Australian-type army hat, the rim curled up at the side like a sneering lip. His arms were usually outstretched, and appeared severed a little below the shoulders as if, just out of shot, they embraced two smiling Burmese girls.

This, at least, was the interpretation that Mr Finkelstein (one of the sheltered) whispered to me as Mrs Salter dutifully and reluctantly passed around the contents of her Ronnie's latest letter home.

Finkelstein, who lived around the corner, had been quick to fill the shelter vacancy created by Ronnie's departure. A confessed coward, he was spending the war years working in a coffin factory. The furniture outlet where he had previously found employment had been requisitioned by the government early in 1941, and Finkelstein, whose sales speciality had been beds, soon found himself preparing customers for eternal rest. In the shelter he was our resident joker: 'Hitler, Mussolini, Goebbels and Himmler are trapped by fire on the top of a high building and forced to jump. Who hits the ground first?' (Silence) 'Who *cares* who hits the ground first?' We would all laugh and Finkelstein would wink leeringly at me.

Mrs Finkelstein, who, through madness or bravery, preferred to remain in her own house during even the worst of the air raids, would put in her appearance some moments after the All Clear had sounded. 'Uh, oh, here comes the trouble and strife,' Finkelstein would say, and his wife would reply, 'Morris, you're a fool.' I never felt that she didn't mean it.

The new addition to our group we called The Silent American, and we were not quite sure how he had come to join us. No one could recall if he had just wandered in one night, or if, as Mrs Salter thought she remembered, he had made his request for shelter while standing behind her in the meat-ration queue. At any rate, he had been with us almost every night for more than a month. He would always arrive a few moments after everyone else and stand, head bent, in the dampest corner of the room. He was enormous, at least to my eyes, and Finkelstein seemed to think so too, for he was forever urging him to take the weight off his feet. There was no way in which standing up could have been comfortable for The Silent

American, but he would never sit down. He was hand-some, clean cut, with straw-blond hair parted at the side, and listless grey eyes that seemed to avoid all contact with the world of things. His uniform, well, his uniform was a problem for me. If he was in the US Air Force, as he seemed to be, then what was he doing with us night after night? I didn't understand. The adults were no help: their glances and dropped voices steadily communicated that such questions as I might have were best left unasked.

As far as our collective fear of air raids was concerned, The Silent American was, undoubtedly, a calming influ-ence. After all, we had our very own pilot right there with us, grounded, of course, but still glowing like an icon in the drab shelter. 'The Presence in the Corner', my mother sometimes called him when she tired of his other name.

Most remarkable of all was the way that the appearance of The Silent American had transformed Mrs Salter. Since his arrival her whole look had changed. Gone were the home-made dresses and cheap sandals that had been the emblems of her wartime thriftiness. In their place were the almost unpurchasable nylons and tight blouses that women usually hoarded for Saturday nights. Gone too were the squares of black-market chocolate that would occasionally come my way. Worst of all, according to my mother, was Mrs Salter's sale of the three chickens that had provided our family with fresh eggs throughout the first two and a half years of the war.

On the night of my eleventh birthday, the Luftwaffe tried to return London to its primordial state, and sink the city's buildings back into the muddy banks of the Thames. The *Evening News* carried a cartoon depicting the East End as a pulsing cockney heart absorbing and diverting bombs as they descended in a black rain from the storm clouds above. There was nothing for it but to hold my party in the shelter. My mother contrived a cake from somewhere, Mr Finkelstein arrived with a bottle of sweet kosher wine. From my father, there were no greetings. In five weeks, he had not uttered a word.

Naturally, the American had been the only one whom my mother had been unable to contact, but when he became aware of the nature of the occasion he was quick to respond. From a deep pocket in his tunic he produced a piece of iron-blue shrapnel, once jagged but now smoothed and buffed, as if intended for a paperweight. The shrapnel seemed to mean a lot to him (why else would he have thought it a worthy present?) and I responded to the gift as if it had been just what I wanted. What I *did* want was my football, but there was no negotiating with Walsh.

When my mother lit the candles the group sang 'Happy Birthday'. Outside, the Germans supplied an accompaniment of booms and flashes to rival Tchaikovsky. For the first time that I could remember we heard the American's voice for more than just a 'Thank you' or 'Goodnight'. And what a voice it was! Even in the rendition of that mundane song his voice stood out like a lark's among blackbirds. 'Sing something else!' Finkelstein enjoined him as soon as I had blown out the tiny flames and, without embarrassment or delay, our Silent American complied. Light and melodious, his voice seemed to take us all to some different imaginary place that I might just as well call 'America'. I was thinking of the giant redwood trees that I had read about in a school geography book, and how they seemed to hold up the sky, like Atlas. Mrs Salter must have been thinking of something quite different, for her eyes filled with tears and, as there was no place for her to run and hide, she simply bent her face forward into her hands and sobbed.

When the song came to an end she stood up abruptly, stepped over to the American, and, with a quick, strong gesture, reached up and pulled his head downwards. What happened next was partly obscured for me by my mother, who, feeling the need to distract me, announced that I had only to turn around to discover my present. Her voice was so deep and intense (as if she too had been transformed by the song) that it served momentarily to draw me away from Mrs Salter. A moment was all that was needed, however, for where the cake had been there now stood, in all its former glory, my battered, mud-encrusted football. I went for it with a cry, and it was a good thirty seconds before I realized that no one was watching me. I followed Finkelstein's gaze back to the corner of the room, and arrived at Mrs Salter and the American detaching themselves from what must have been a passionate embrace. The onlookers, myself excepted, chose to behave as if nothing untoward had occurred to upset the natural order of the universe.

For the next few nights, despite my protestations, my mother insisted that we sit out the air raids in the cupboard under the stairs. One snowy night, when, because of poor visibility, the Germans desisted for a while, we took the bus to the hospital to visit my father. The journey, although it was only a few miles, seemed interminable. The bus inched down slippery streets, past semi-detached suburban houses, some of which had their windows blown out, or the wooden rafters of their roofs poking through. In the front garden of one house a bomb had fallen deeply into the soft soil, sending most of its blast harmlessly upward. The house was intact, the red slates secure on the roof, the windows in place, but the garden looked like a chaotic archaeological dig. The snow, meanwhile, was turning the mountain of mud into a wintry peak. Two children, poorly dressed for the cold, hatless and gloveless, but wild-eyed and excited, waved at me from their summit as we drove past.

My mother and I arrived forty-five minutes into the visiting hour. We dropped our gasmasks, in their clumsy, cylindrical cases, beside my father's bed, and prepared for our customary vigil. My father was sitting up staring at the opposite wall. For weeks, my mother had chatted through these hours as if my father were responding. She would report the day's events, filling him in on war news and local gossip. From time to time she would urge me to relate some incident from my school life. At first I had complied, and I had tried to make my stories as interesting as possible by putting into my voice the 'expression' that my mother so much admired in the voices of her favourite dramatic actors. But now, after so many fruitless hours, the narrative of my escapades came out in a halting, cracked voice that faded into silence before the story was half finished. On this night, my mother sent me to wander round the ward to entertain, with my youthful presence, some of the other poor souls, most of whom were suffering from some form or other of Blitz fatigue. One man repeated his name and address to me, another asked if I were going to marry Hetty, and why I had run off with Judy, and then dumped her. At the end of my rounds I returned to my father's bedside. My mother, in desperation I believe, was telling her most precious story, the one that, up until now, she would not tell in front of me – the story of The Silent American and Mrs Salter. Acknowledging my presence with a glance, my mother described my birthday party and the embrace. I wasn't sure if I imagined it but my father's eyes seemed to show a flicker of interest.

'He's from Omaha, Nebraska,' my mother said, in the slow register she used when speaking to foreigners. 'His name,' and here she paused to indicate that something momentous was coming, 'is Nathanael Dodge III.' There was a long silence. At the far end of the room the nursing sister rose from her desk and announced that visiting time was over. She switched the ceiling lights off and on; my father's face flickered in the sickly orange light.

'The third?' said my father. 'Is he royalty?'

Even more than the happy astonishment of my father speaking, it was the magic of 'Omaha, Nebraska' that drew my passionate attention. From this moment, it seemed to me, whatever worlds I might conjure, these words would be my incantation. With 'Omaha, Nebraska' the walls of the hospital ward collapsed, and the flickering lights in the room gave way to a lambent dawn over a distant prairie.

Early the next morning, a Sunday, I took my football out into the street for a kickabout. The snow had laid a thin carpet of white over the pavement. I ran up the street etching a zig-zag of passes against the walls of my neighbours' houses. When I approachd the crater I crashed a shot as hard as I could into the grey winter sky. I knew that my ball would disappear into the deep hole, and that retrieving it would require a tricky but entertaining descent. Approaching at a run, I peered down from the edge, and saw, not my ball, but The Silent American. He stood stiffly, almost at attention, his arms by his sides, and his back pressed against the crater wall. 'Omaha,' I said quietly, and more to myself than to him. My football lay two or three feet in front of him. It seemed that he could not move. We stood looking at each other for about a minute. Finally he took a deep breath and said, 'Stay there, I'll throw it up.' He reached quickly to the ball, lobbed it into my hands, then moved swiftly back to the mud wall.

What I said next were words from a child to a child. I asked him if he 'wanted to play'. He did. I wasn't surprised. After all, the previous night I had heard my mother describe Nathanael to my father as 'only a boy', and there was a great deal of the gangly fourteen-year-old left in his long-limbed airman's splendour.

We walked quickly to the nearby park. Once there, settled on a wide field that the train tracks bisected, I sidefooted the ball to my American, and waited for returns. They never came. Instead, Nathanael Dodge would collect my passes into his hands and punt them high above the snow-lined trees. When the leather orb descended I would trap it deftly with my foot, and send it skidding across the frozen grass back to his waiting hands. We continued in this way for about an hour, each of us playing our own sport, until a distant flurry of activity around the Nissen huts brought an abrupt end to the game. When three soldiers manoeuvring a gun into position became clearly visible, Nathanael said, 'Gotta go,' and ran towards the park gates.

Did I know then that he was both wanted and pursued? I suppose I did, but, in the absence of my father, my loneliness and fear were such that I was not about to let the crime of desertion come between me and a new friendship. In any case, in my mind at that time, half-acknowledged as the shadow of a truth, there was only one deserter worthy of the name: Lewis Gilchrist, the father who had removed himself from our house, who had fallen into silence, and who was threatening, through the unmanageable weakness of his heart, to abandon me altogether.

In the next few weeks, in counterpoint to my visits to the hospital, where my father, although he now spoke occasionally, remained locked in a depressive state, I found myself the cheerful companion of the no-longer-silent American. If the nights belonged to Mrs Salter and her passion, the days, after school, belonged to me. Nathanael Dodge and I would hike to some far corner of Gladstone Park, where, shivering in the chill January winds, I would listen enthralled to his tales of high school, baseball, and the girls back home.

Our favourite resting spot was a deserted ornamental garden set on a slope of the park's highest hill. Left untended during the war, this garden provided benches to sit on, and a surrounding brick wall to ward off the worst of winter. At its central point had been set a white stone sundial, narrow paths ran out from its base, like the rays on the Japanese flag with which I was so familiar.

It was here, one white, mournful day, looking over the evergreen shrubs, dwarf hedges, broken boughs, and uncollected garden waste scattered in the mud, that we

told each other our darkest secrets. What I had to report
was confused anger and embarrassment at my father's
predicament, feelings that had been bottled up inside me
ever since the night of the imaginary fire.

For almost as long as I had known him, I had been
aware that my father's health was fragile. When he and I
would walk in the park, on what were grandly called
'nature rambles' (this meant that we carried with us a
brown paper bag to collect leaves and acorns), my father
would have to pause for breath halfway up the smoothest
incline. I would hold his arm while he inhaled deeply and
prepared to move on. Often, he would pretend that we
had stopped to observe a bird in flight, or the afternoon
steam train approaching down the tracks. On the night
of the fire, however, his muscles were iron and his energy
boundless. Used to being overwhelmed by his weakness,
I now found myself overcome by his strength. What did
it all mean? Why didn't my father ever try to explain to
me what was happening to him? My mother, I knew, was
distracted, by the war, by the need to scrape by, by the
thousand and one demands of daily life.

Under an ice-blue sky, Nathanael Dodge listened carefully to my story. With his fingers, he turned over a flower
marker that a gardener had left on a path, no doubt during
the last hours of his pre-war work: the word 'Foxglove'
accompanied by a faded picture of dotted purple tubular
flowers rested in the palm of his hand.

'Your father,' he finally told me, 'loves you very much.'

'Well he doesn't show it,' I said. 'He won't even speak
to me.'

'Where did he go first?' Nathanael asked.

'What do you mean?'

'In the fire, where did he go first? He went to pull *you*
out of bed, he went to *save* you.'

'But there was no fire,' I argued foolishly.

'There was,' said Nathanael. 'For him, there was. You
know that.'

In return, he told me about his fear, the night missions he had flown, the point of no return that he had reached one day when the call came to scramble. How he had indeed 'scrambled', but on his hands and knees, and in the opposite direction, through a hedgerow, out of the base, towards – where? Anywhere.

This was our last conversation. Two nights later, on the night of a full moon, when the blackout seemed as futile as the guns in the park, my mother and I were once more obliged to cross the road for shelter. Before we had even arrived at our front gate we were waved back by a white-helmeted soldier. I had compiled a scrapbook of uniforms and was quick to recognize the tunic of the US Military Police. After a few moments we heard a cry, and then three shadowy figures appeared at the foot of the Salters' garden path.

He came slowly towards us flanked by two bobbing white heads, and he arrived in the full glare of the moon-light opposite my mother and me. I was hoping he would speak, but he was back in his silence, where we had first met him. As the soldiers marched him off around the corner I called out 'Omaha! Omaha!' but the magic didn't work. Mrs Salter appeared at the door of the shelter, ghostly in a white nightdress. A small crowd had formed in her driveway. I don't know if she heard Walsh shout, 'Bastard, got what he deserved,' but she turned quickly at the sound of his voice, and rushed into her darkened, unprotected house.

A week later my father came home. He entered the house tentatively, sheepishly. He was wearing a heavy herringbone overcoat and a trilby hat with an inappropri-ately jaunty feather stuck in the band. He kept his coat on while he drank tea at the kitchen table. For a while he didn't speak, and I feared that the hospital's assurances of his recovery had been premature. Finally, he looked at my mother and outlined slowly and clearly the adjust-ments that had been made to his medication. It was hoped that there would be no more hallucinations, no more side-effects. He concluded by saying, 'I'm sorry, Rachel.' He tried then, very hard, to look me in the eyes, but his shame had too powerful a grip. Instead, he pulled me to him. Pressed against his chest, hearing his irregular heart thump in its bony cage, I tried to say that there was really nothing for him to be sorry about, but I didn't have the words.

Shoes

that it was all

If you are going to think about love then you might as well be on the island of Cyprus. After all, it was here that Aphrodite first blasted out of the sea in a cloud of surf. When I arrived, in the summer of 1989, I was in retreat from love, or something that had resembled it. So at first the eruptions of the wine-dark sea, and the deep feelings that they engendered, appeared inappropriate. Then someone told me another version of the myth. The goddess, I learned, might have sprung from seawater that had been uncannily impregnated by Uranus's severed and discarded genitals. Now this was a love-vision worth pondering.

I came to Cyprus in the first place because of Mr Shemesh. And because after a love affair breaks up you tend to have time on your hands, and lots of 'new ideas'. Mine were about cycling. I suppose, really, that it was all about getting rid of surplus energy. But also, the desire for fresh air. Career downhill, traverse the forest, pass the scented pines and fruity carob. Yes, she is gone, but, lo, the winter is past, and a few deep breaths might (*might*) put you back in business.

So I went down to this little store on Agron Street and checked out the shiny, fat-tyred, eighteen-speed mountain bikes; imports, of course, from Japan and the USA. 'Light as air,' shouted a man in overalls from the back of the shop. 'Aluminium. And with granny gears. You could cross the Alps.'

I left and went to see Shemesh. He looked at me across his desk as if stupidity was my middle name. 'Why don't you buy a car?' he asked. 'No one in Jerusalem uses a bicycle. The city is too hilly. Up, down.' He traced alpine contours in the air with his hand. 'A car is what you need.'

We were in his tiny office, no more than a cubicle really, in the Customs Building. It was hot. I had waited two hours to see him. 'I can't afford a car,' I replied, 'and anyway, that's not the point. I want to buy a bicycle. It's a personal thing.' (This phrase, I knew, had almost no meaning in Israel.) 'I would like you to sign the import tax release form. I'm entitled to an exemption.'

'Let me have another look at your passport,' said Shemesh. I handed it over. 'It says here,' he continued, 'that you are a Visiting Foreign Expert.' I gave him an affirmative nod. 'What exactly are you an expert in?'

'Advanced Missile Detection.'

Shemesh gave me a long look. The fan on his desk whooshed cool air into his face. I wanted to lean forward, and bang down the oscillation button.

'Okay,' I said, 'I'm sorry, I shouldn't be facetious. I'm an artist. Right now I'm working on the Zeitlin Project.' Would he ask me to go further? I hoped not. Zeitlin was my friend, Henry Zeitlin, who had urged me to come and stay with him for a few weeks, eight years earlier. Thanks to an immense foul-up at the Israeli embassy in London, I had been granted a long-term VFE visa instead of the normal six-month tourist affair. The project, if Zeitlin and I ever had one, was meeting women.

'What is the Zeitlin Project?'

'Murals' (pause) 'for children' (longer pause) 'in playgrounds all over the city.' I started to loosen up. 'You know the Golem slide at Kiryat Yovel? Like that, only on walls. Zeitlin designs them – it's a municipality contract – and I execute the paintings.' Before Shemesh could ask, 'Why you?' I added that I had done a number of such works in England before coming to Israel. Shemesh thought for a moment. I made a movement up and down with my right hand, as if I were holding a large brush, and smoothly obliterating an ugly section of Jerusalem wall. All this for a two-thousand-shekel tax rebate.

'All right, you can have your privilege,' said Shemesh, starting to rustle through some papers on his desk. 'But you will have to take the bicycle out of the country, within ten days, then bring it back in. You must enter, you see, with the bicycle.'

'You're kidding.'

'That's the law,' Shemesh went on. 'You're lucky that such a loophole exists. We are slowly closing them all.' I calculated in my head how much the ferry to and from Cyprus would cost me (Egypt, a bureaucratic nightmare, was out of the question).

'Do you know how much money I'm going to have to spend?' I asked Shemesh. 'It's ridiculous.'

Shemesh threw up his hands, and spun two full turns in his swivel chair. He returned from his second orbit in a very bad mood. 'Never mind you.' He could barely subdue the anger in his voice. 'What about me? Suppose I, an Israeli, a person who was born here, a person who has been in the army, a person with a *wound*' (he pointed vaguely towards his chest), 'suppose I wanted to buy one of these mountain bikes. I would have to sell my house first. But you, because of a lucky stamp in a passport, get a bicycle, a day trip, and money left over. What is more, you should be ashamed. A Jew, posing as a Visiting Foreigner.' He threw four sheets of paper across the desk; the carbons caught in the jet stream from the fan and fluttered pleasantly, like big ink-stained butterflies. 'Sign here. The yellow is for me. The pink is for you. The white is for upstairs, the other white is for at the port.'

I was a bad sailor, so I took two Dramamine before getting on the boat. The pills made no difference. Almost as soon as we pulled out of Haifa I threw up over the side, then I sat, pale and still, registering every wave on the seismograph of my stomach. The journey took seven hours.

I had planned, in order to annoy Shemesh, to wait on the boat in Limassol while it turned around. But my equilibrium was shot, and the island of Cyprus, all pink and white in the dawn light, looked so inviting that I decided to disembark and explore the harbour. I made my way over to a beach-front taverna and ordered breakfast. The waiter brought coffee, pitta bread, feta cheese, and crumple-skinned black olives. I was beginning to enjoy myself. For half an hour I watched gulls wheel and dip, and white-sailed dinghies tack out towards the horizon. Then, *they* appeared.

I saw Rose first. She was wearing an embroidered peasant shirt, and a long, black, gauzy skirt. She was barefoot. Her long, coppery hair was pulled back from her face, and tied up in a bun, Greek-goddess style. The man accompanying her was very tall, with short red hair, and a lot of freckles.

Rose and I spotted each other at about the same time. I tried to stay calm, despite the tachycardia that I was experiencing. She squeezed her companion's arm, whispered something to him, and came over to my table. 'Before you say anything,' she said, 'I want to tell you that I just got married.'

'Excuse me,' I replied, spitting an olive pit into the palm of my hand, 'but don't I know you? Didn't we recently break up?'

'Sam' (there was a 'please don't do this' pitch in her voice), 'that was months ago. I haven't seen you for *nine months*.' I looked at her, she had this nice Aegean-gold tan, different from her normal Mediterranean-brown. Or was I simply noting the auriferous glow that surrounds a happy honeymooner? 'My husband's name' (husband!) 'is Carl Lund.' Rose gestured back over her shoulder; the giant's shadow was approaching. 'He's from Minnesota.'

'I can see that,' I said. I could also see why she was in Cyprus. Like me, she had slipped through a loophole. A Jew can't marry a gentile in the land of Israel.

The last time I had seen Rose was outside Jaffa Gate in Jerusalem. We had gone our separate ways, she into another relationship, and me into monkdom and misery. As time passed, one kind friend or another would tell me with whom she was living now, or with whom she had just broken up. I already knew about Megged, a flora and fauna specialist. He had been followed by Yoav, a keeper at the Biblical Zoo (two of every animal named in the Bible), and Yoram who taught agronomics at the Haifa Technion. Rose loved Nature types. Now it seemed she had found Carl.

The new husband was upon us. 'Glad to meet you,' he said, shaking my hand, and giving me this big, friendly smile. 'You going back on the boat?' I didn't reply. After a few awkward moments – they ordered coffee, I said I had to be getting along, they half-urged me to stay, I said 'no, no', that sort of thing – Carl got up to go to the bathroom.

'Well,' I began, but Rose cut me off.

'Carl's a very kind person.'

'Oh, good,' I replied, 'that's important.'

Rose ignored me. 'He's a tree surgeon, there's Dutch Elm disease all the way down from Jerusalem to Sha'ar Hagai. The Forestry Department brought him over.'

So Carl was a real Visiting Foreign Expert. I was impressed, and envious. Rose smiled at me. She had wonderful straight white teeth, the long-term benefit of an American childhood and sophisticated early orthodontic care.

'We were on the islands, Mykonos, Limnos, then we went to Rhodes, then we came back here. We spent last week up in the Troodos. You can't imagine how beautiful it is. Mountain chapels. Oil lamps burning through the summer nights.' I must have assumed my disdainful/ indifferent look because Rose said, 'Be nice, Sam, you can be, you know. Sometimes you have to take a chance. You and I . . .' Her voice trailed off. I remembered Zeitlin introducing us at a Purim party. Rose had been dressed as an angel (she was young), gossamer wings, white flowers in her hair, while I, by odd coincidence, had arrived as a fallen angel, with bruised face and broken wings. We danced all night while this great bang of orange blossom came in through the open windows. It had seemed like a match made in heaven.

'Lundy,' Rose called out, 'we're over here.' Big Lundy, who had been walking in the wrong direction, lumbered back towards us.

I said, 'Don't you think you should have waited? After all, marriage is a serious business. It is not something that you rush into. You need to think it all through. Actions have consequences.' I had never counselled before. Rose knew this, and looked at me as if I were quite mad.

Away to our left, Lundy had stopped in mid-stride; some phenomenon in the world of nature, maybe a fellow tree-trunk, had taken his attention. Rose wasn't going to let me off. 'Face it, Sam, we didn't work as a couple. You were ambivalent right up to the moment when I decided to let it all go. In any case, you're not a long-haul person. You're good at breakfast, which is something, most men aren't, but by lunchtime you're already restless. And another thing . . .' I held my hand up. I didn't want to hear about sexual selfishness, and I saw that the subject was making a fast approach down the tracks.

'Okay,' I said, 'I know.'

'No,' she replied, 'You don't know. Orgasms are important to me, you were always impatient.'

I fell silent. Rose reached out towards me; I thought, for a moment, that she was going to caress my cheek, but she said, 'You have feta cheese in your beard,' and brushed the offending specks away.

What could I do? She was married to Minnesota. The sun was beginning to heat up, and port activity to increase. The hull of a ferry boat opened; a line of cars bumped down a wooden ramp. Lundy said, 'Look, little teeth leaving an open jaw.' I smiled. Rose told me (as if I wanted to know) about their plans to return to America.

Lundy was called wherever trees were in trouble. After Israel, it seemed, he was wanted in Alaska. I had a mental flash of *tundra*, log cabin, smoke rising from the chimney. One thing was for sure, there was no way I was going back on that boat with them.

They boarded the ferry. I waved, regally, from the quay. A storm, I thought, bring on a tempest. Sink the boat, but save her. I looked up at lofty, strong Lundy, leaning on the deck rail, grinning and waving. Oh, these were bad, evil thoughts. But the allegations of sexual monocentrism had stung. I suppose I wanted revenge.

I rode south-west along a coastal road. Every now and then I stopped to buy a drink. I was very pleased with the pace of my journey. At bicycle speed, the sky was definitely bluer, the beaches whiter, the foam on the churning sea foamier. You see, Shemesh? I thought. Who needs a car?

The problem with not going back on the boat was that I would miss the thirty-fifth-birthday party Zeitlin was throwing for himself. Zeitlin had got in with a fast crowd, movie people, acquaintances of Golan and Globus. He had promised me a rare assortment of introductions. I was hoping, of course, to end my sexual drought, and to dive again into the turbulent, but not necessarily unpleasant, waters of love.

Zeitlin was my oldest friend from London. His parents had taken him off to Israel, after the Six Day War, when we were both in our late teens. When I first arrived in Jerusalem, we had spent hours walking around the city. Zeitlin took me to all his secret places: the Turkish Baths inside the Dung Gate, a Chinese restaurant in a gas station, the pitta bakery on the corner of Narkiss Street. This last stop was my favourite. Two thick-armed, flour-covered men spread thin layers of dough on round scatter cushions, then they slammed the cushions against the concave walls of open clay ovens. The dough stuck, spread and rose. We would stand on a street corner, eat the hot bread, and observe the morning's bustle and commotion.

The subject, on our philosophical rambles, was love. Zeitlin was always falling in love. And when he did, the relationship, for a few weeks anyway, was always perfect, passionate, distinctive and exceptional. I was not then so interested in the topic as I am now. And I was impatient with his obsessions. I didn't listen when he said things to me like 'Have you noticed that people who are happy in love have a look of profound concentration which is almost indistinguishable from a look of profound sadness?' Later, when things started to fall apart with Rose, I came to regret my inattentiveness.

Back in the seventies Zeitlin and I had wanted to live life on the edge. We had tried to resist permanent jobs and stultifying institutions. I had talent as a painter, but very little confidence; Zeitlin's situation was more or less the reverse. We had hoped that wandering around, a kind of vagabondage with regular meals, might compensate for the attributes we lacked. It didn't. In the long run, Zeitlin fell into the money pit, and became a market analyst. He remained, however, my closest confidant. The person I turned to in times of crisis. What was I supposed to do about the fact that I couldn't get over Rose? Zeitlin, and Zeitlin's party, might have provided all the answers.

So, it was hard for me to pass up the return trip from Cyprus, especially when I knew that I had done so out of jealousy and foolishness.

In the late afternoon I arrived in Paphos, and checked into a small hotel. I took a bath (the water came out brown, then eased to rust) and popped a couple of muscle relaxants I had borrowed from a friend in anticipation of bike-ache. In the early evening I wandered around the town. It was pretty dead. A few young girls, giggling and holding hands with each other, seemed to be on my circuit. They were shadowed, at a distance of about twenty yards, by two squat, silent chaperones, dressed in black. At intervals we would pass solitary men, in grimy vests and shiny trousers, closing up shop. They would stop what they were doing, turn their heads, and watch the girls until the escort service came into view. Courtship looked like a tough proposition. On the other hand, perhaps if someone other than me had been arranging and controlling my love life all these years, things might have gone better.

One more turn around the square, a jink left past the post office, then down to the waterfront. Here, on the dirty littoral, behind a dilapidated warehouse, I came across a children's playground. I went and sat in one of the patched and peeling cars of the kiddy-carousel. Where were Aphrodite's progeny? Where was the seafront garden of delight? More important, where was my sweater? I was starting to shiver. Now if Rose had been here . . . No use. Back at the hotel I had read in a tourist guide about a black stone, an idol of Aphrodite, that had been discovered in a Paphos cowshed. Young women desperate for love visited the shrine. They ripped ribbons from their petticoats, lay them down, went home and waited for a response. Perhaps in the morning I could bike out there, leave a pair of cotton underpants, hope for the best.

I walked back towards the hotel. Halfway down a narrow street, an open doorway released a rectangle of white light. Above it was a sign in the shape of a shoe. I approached and peered in. A cobbler was bent over his bench, piercing small holes in a leather upper. He paused in his work, and turned towards me.

'You work late,' I said.

'Yes,' he replied. 'Come in, come in.'

The room, illuminated by a naked light-bulb, was hung with shoe-trees and cobbler's tools. The cobbler wore a full-length leather apron. He smiled at me, showing a row of uneven, broken teeth. The light clarified the shine on his bald head, brightened his broad, fleshy nose and watery grey eyes. He had a small awl in his hand but when I entered he replaced it in a loop of his leather belt.

'Coffee? You will take coffee?'

I nodded a thank you.

'Greek coffee. We say *Greek* coffee now. Since the Turks. You know. I will make you *Greek* coffee.'

I sat at his workbench while he heated up the coffee on a two-ring gas range. Then he disappeared into the back of his shop to fetch sugar, spoons and two small cups. 'From where?' he asked, still smiling at me and nodding his head approvingly.

'From Israel.'

Ah. Usually this brought conversation up short, the interlocutor would do a little moral accounting, then proceed in a different direction. But my host simply broadened his smile.

'Ben Gurion,' he said, 'very good. Shamir, very bad.' It was my turn to wag my head up and down. He heaped two sugars into his cup while I covered mine. 'Solomos,' he said, 'Fotis Solomos.'

'Sam, Samuel Solomons.'

He looked at me as if he hadn't quite heard me properly. Then we both started to laugh.

Fotis Solomos showed me the different kinds of awls and hammers that he used. Then he led me to a rack of tanned skins hung in a side room. 'Feel, feel the leather.' Then he took down a framed letter from a British Member of Parliament. It was typed on House of Commons stationery and said: 'Dear Mr Solomos. I cannot tell you how pleased I am with the shoes. They are absolutely splendid.' There were more letters: from an American businessman, from a colonel at the local British army base, from a German tourist. 'Would you like?' Solomos pointed at my feet. 'Would you also like?'

I demurred on the shoes but, after two hours of friendly conversation ('You mean you actually draw round people's feet?' 'Look for yourself. I will show you my book.') I was happy to accept a late-lunch invitation to Solomos's home for the following day.

Back at the hotel I sat in my room, drank a small bottle of ouzo, and reflected, This is the way to make friends. Chance meetings. Odd moments plucked from a random fate. I won't say that I didn't also send a few thoughts across to that other place in the sun where Rose and Carl were probably, at that very moment, shrugging off tiredness to go at one another in post-honeymoon abandon. Were there things she and I hadn't thought of? Brachiation. He was a tree-man, after all. Was there a wild, ragged swinging in their bedroom? Mid-air coupling? *Unselfish* mid-air coupling? But even jealousy tends to be tempered by fatigue. And I was too weary to torture myself for long. With the windows flung open I could hear the sea, my other enemy, sliding up on the beach. At least my stomach, if not my heart, was back to normal. I went to sleep.

Solomos and I ate together on the next two days. For some reason he never seemed to want to leave his home. Sometimes while I was there, a woman would turn up with groceries, or a man would come by with sausage, or a bottle of wine. But the visitors never stayed long. In fact, Solomos seemed oddly friendless. He told me that he enjoyed meeting foreigners, especially the British. He loved the English language, he wanted to practise with me, also to read and write. The other townspeople were provincial, no yearning for the wide world. They lived inside narrow boundaries.

I was beginning to enjoy my solitude, and my new friend. In the mornings I would cycle down to the empty beach and swim, then go and sit in one of the street cafés. Nobody bothered me. Groups of men sat around on low chairs, idle, but not, it seemed, unhappy.

On the third day, after a lunchtime siesta, I made my way, as usual, to Solomos's place. When I got there he began to quiz me about where exactly I lived in Israel. I described my Jerusalem neighbourhood, and he seemed pleased. After we had eaten, he asked me if I would mind going upstairs to meet his wife. He had told me when we first met that she was ill, temporarily confined to bed.

Mrs Solomos was propped up in bed on two enormous, hand-embroidered pillows. She had a thin face and wavy grey hair combed over to cover a bald patch. Her eyes were closed. On the white wall above her head hung a large wooden crucifix. Her bedside table, covered with medicine bottles, also displayed a syringe in a plastic kidney bowl. Late afternoon light, pale lemon, strained through the shutters.

She woke up. As soon as she opened her sharp, blue eyes and spotted her husband, she began to scream. My Greek was hopeless, but certain words were clearly repeated: *'pezavengi'*, *'pushti'*. Solomos, flushing red, moved quickly to the bedside and tried to calm her. 'Eleni,' he said, and clasped her bony hands. He began to murmur in her ear. She continued to scream. 'Please,' he said in English. 'We have a guest, from Jerusalem.'

There was something about the way Solomos stressed the name of the city, his infusion of awe and holiness, that should have alerted me to what was coming. It certainly had the desired effect on Eleni. She calmed down, and gave me a hard look. Solomos continued: 'I thought, a prayer. He can go for you, he can make a prayer.' So that was it. He wanted me to be a messenger to God in His omphalos.

But Mrs Solomos was less enthusiastic than her husband had hoped. 'For me? What about for you? He should say a hundred prayers for you, a hundred thousand. Or doesn't he know? I see from his face that he doesn't know.' She turned her attention to me. 'You. Do you know how to pray?' My impulse was to recite the Hebrew blessings over wine and bread, but I restrained myself, and merely shrugged. 'Can you say Kyrie Eleison?'

I looked over at Solomos; he signalled with his eyes that I should respond affirmatively. 'I can learn,' I said.

We went back down to the workshop. Solomos filled his mouth with tacks and started to resole a shoe. 'Okay,' I said, 'what's the story? What don't I know?' He kept hammering for a few moments, then suddenly spat the remaining tacks onto the floor.

'Sometimes women come in here,' he looked towards the door as if one might enter at this very moment. 'They sit. They want boots. I measure.'

'I see.' I did see. I saw it all: Solomos kneeling, the faint rasp of stocking against his stubbly cheek, his deft cobbler's fingers working their way upwards into soft flesh.

Solomos sighed. 'One came. More than half my age. I don't know why she was interested. But she was. It's a small town. Now she walks around with a big belly.'

Oh, wonderful. What have we got here? A sick wife, a pregnant teenager, an inconstant shoemaker, and a spurned lover. O Solomos. O Solomons. All the earth seeks to hear your wisdom. For wisdom is better than rubies.

I wasn't at all sure that I could manage the prayer. I said, 'I'm really no good in churches. I get claustrophobic, and the incense gives me a headache.'

Solomos asked, 'What about synagogues?'

'The same,' I replied, 'except for the incense.'

'How about outdoors? Somewhere in Jerusalem. A holy place?'

'There's the Wall. The Wailing Wall. You must know about that, it's what remains of Herod's temple. Orthodox Jews pray there. Some leave messages in the cracks. Messages to God.'

Solomos's eyes lit up. 'I'll give you a message,' he said excitedly, 'a prayer for her. You won't even have to say anything, you can just make the deposit. I must end this business. I must straighten things out.' He grabbed a handful of nails, and began to bang them into the shoe with tremendous force.

As Solomos worked, I remembered a poem that I had given Rose shortly before deciding that I wanted to spend a lifetime with her. It read 'As sole is to shoe/ So I am to you.' I had meant it as an expression of profound connectedness. Suddenly, it seemed to carry a different message: I am what you walk on.

Back at the hotel I took a rust shower then changed into a new pair of jeans. In the back pocket was the invitation to Zeitlin's party. What was I doing here? I could have attended a crowded, noisy party, with high-quality marijuana and attractive women. Instead of music and excitement, I had chosen blankness: whitewashed walls and scrubbed doorsteps. I scrutinized the invitation. Could that 3 in 13th by an 8? If so, the party was the next day, a Saturday, of course, not a Monday! This was wish fulfilment, but maybe not, and even if I was wrong, Zeitlin was bound to be holding one of his regular Saturday-night sessions. I could go back, begin again, be a lace to someone's eye, a tongue to their throat.

On our last day together Solomos asked me, no, begged me, to let him make me a pair of shoes. I agreed, but only if he would allow me to pay for them at the regular price. We argued for a while. I explained that I wouldn't feel right taking a gift in exchange for a prayer. At first Solomos was insistent, but eventually he relented. He asked me for one hundred and twenty-five Cyprus pounds. I was a little surprised at the amount. But I was not about to quibble over money. Solomos would get what I had saved on the bicycle tax.

He handed me a pencil and told me to write my forwarding address in the middle of a page in his huge ledger. Then, he asked me to take my shoes and socks off. I placed my feet on facing pages, my right foot concealing my address. Solomos drew two podiatral outlines.

I stepped back and admired the shape of my feet.

Solomos led me towards the rack of hides. 'Choose,' he said. I fingered a soft buckskin.

'For a wedding?' Solomos asked.

'Not mine,' I replied. He indicated that, in that case, the creamy buckskin was inappropriate. I went with it nevertheless. From a glossy catalogue I selected a stylish, if conservative, design.

I couldn't face cycling back to Limassol so I took the bus instead. In the terminal, on the seafront, Fotis and I shook hands and hugged. Over his shoulder I saw two pelicans diving for fish, their baggy jaws wide open and ready to scoop. He handed me the prayer. It was a cigarette-sized scroll with a floral design; a scrap of wallpaper tightened with an elastic band.

I got back to Jerusalem (four Dramamine, two muscle relaxants) in the early evening, tired, but ready to party. It was a warm night. Zeitlin's house was at the bottom of a long hill, not far from my place. I thought I'd coast down to the party on my bike, leave it overnight, and pick it up in the morning.

When I pedalled out onto the street a bunch of local kids came out to admire my purchase. I stopped so they could perform a quick inspection. They plucked the spokes as if they were harp strings, and rolled their 'r's around 'granny gears' in wonder and awe.

I approached Zeitlin's expecting to hear music bursting through the open windows, and hoping to see people spilled out onto the small lawn in front of his building. Instead, the only person I saw was Rose, alone, coming through the front door. Her face was pale, and when she saw me her eyes registered nothing at all. 'Oh, Sam,' she said, abstractedly. 'We wondered when you'd come.'

'Where is everybody?' I asked. Could I have got the wrong night again? Rose looked as if she were going to cry, but she held back.

'He's dead,' she said (Lundy!), 'Zeitlin's dead. I told his mother I'd come by and clear out a few things.'

Zeitlin had come off the basketball court feeling pains in his chest. Before he could get to a doctor he had suffered a massive heart attack. He was thirty-five. I couldn't at all begin to process what had happened. This was my best friend. We had a *future* together. There was unfinished business. A lot of it.

I didn't see Rose again, choosing instead to mourn with other friends. I paid a condolence call to Zeitlin's parents; when I shook hands with his father his fingers felt so thin and brittle I thought they might break in my grip.

It was a few weeks before I could bring myself to fulfil my Cyprus assignment. I was angry with God, and didn't want to be anywhere near his possible presence. Then, late one afternoon, I had to make a trip to the Old City to pick up some canvas, so I went down to the Wall. I stood in the glaring sun, my face pressed close to the huge stones. I had the prayer clutched in my hand. Then, I did a terrible thing. I opened the message. It said: MAKE MY WIFE DIE. Next to me a bearded Hasid mumbled speedy prayers and shifted from side to side. O god of gods, I thought, was this a prayer for divine mercy, or divine murder?

I pocketed the paper. But a dreadful curiosity had come over me. What was everybody thinking? I had to know. I had waved to Lundy, but I wanted him drowned. As for Solomos, hadn't I seen him whisper in his wife's ear, hadn't I heard him yearn for forgiveness?

When the Hasid closed his eyes to pray, I pressed my fingers into the Wall's fissures and extracted message after message. I stuffed my pockets with them, and, with the sun sinking behind my back, rode home.

I spread the tiny scrolls out on my kitchen table. They were written in a variety of tongues and directed, to my surprise, to a slew of Gods. All the major religions were represented. Three began 'Dear Jesus,' two were for Allah (in English). Most, like Solomos's, had no named addressee. Sick relatives needed a lot of help, and people who had lost their money. One person had written: 'Give me a woman' but sex, in general, was a minority concern. There were several messages for the dead.

I sat with my stack, full of shame and confusion. What did people want? It was all so banal and predictable. They wanted what they couldn't have: health forever, love forever, God's curse on their enemies, His blessing on their loved ones, a wife taken out of the picture!

A year later, when I had long since given up hope, my shoes arrived. I removed them from their tissue wrapping. They were brown, and clunky. I had seen the men who frequented cafés in Paphos wear shoes just like these. For them, they were good, sturdy, walking shoes, and they might have been for me too, if they had fitted. Solomos's custom-made shoes were at least a size too small.

I searched in the wrapping and came up with a post-card. On one side was a picture of a pelican, on the other Solomos had written me a note. He hoped I enjoyed the shoes. With luck I would visit Cyprus again. Oh, and, almost an afterthought, had I remembered to put his prayer in the Wall? His wife had died a week after I left. He was lonelier than he ever imagined he would be. The girl's family would not let him see the baby.

I think I understood the message of the shoes, or, at least, this is what I thought. Death, when it comes, never fits. You go along with your life, you make plans, the plans involve other people. Then death comes, and nothing fits. Sometimes it squeezes you, sometimes it gives you too much room.

Paris Nights

Charlie Posner has taken out an injunction against his partner's wife, Annette. She's not allowed to visit his office, or telephone him there. She's not permitted to call him at home. If she sees Charlie on the street, or in a restaurant, or at the cinema, she has to keep her distance. Leon, Annette's husband, sympathizes with Charlie. In fact, he is so fed up with his wife that he has instructed his secretary not to put her calls through to him except in the case of an emergency.

Leon, of course, can phone Annette as often as he likes, but he is a creature of habit and sticks to the three-o'clock call that he has made every working day for the last ten years. It doesn't matter where he is, in an important meeting, or chatting with one of the junior staff, he looks at his watch, says 'Omigod,' and rushes into his office. Charlie says Leon always has to go to the bathroom after checking in at home. He cleans his glasses with soap and water, then returns to work.

I've known them all a long time, Charlie, Annette, and Leon. Annette held my mother's arm, sobbing, when we three boys went off to Paris to survey the aftermath of May 1968. Annette cried and waved a huge bunch of coral roses that Leon had refused to take on the train with him. Even my mother, who in her conservatory way always regarded passion as a waste of energy, like fire left burning in an empty room, could see that Annette was a person of sensitivity and deep feeling.

'Goodbye Pumpkin!' Annette yelled as the guard began to slam the doors. Leon nearly fell out of the window.

'Don't ever call me that in front of these two again,' he said. We called him 'Pumpkin' for the rest of the summer.

If you are to understand the current crisis you have to know what happened that summer. For it was then, on that dusty London platform twenty-four years earlier, that the long yearning began which is the cause of all the trouble.

The guard blew his whistle and Leon went off to the toilet. Quick as a flash, Charlie was out on the platform. Through the fogged-up windows of the train, I saw him press something into Annette's hand.

'What was that?' I asked when he jumped back into our carriage.

'Nothing,' he replied.

As we pulled away, Annette stood anchored on my mother's arm. Later, she told me that if she had let go she would have floated up to the rafters of Victoria Station, roses in hand.

On the ferry from Dover to Calais we helped a Japanese girl who was throwing up over the side. The wind was blowing her vomit back into her face, so Charlie turned her round and wiped off her clothes. Her name was Mitzki, but Charlie called her *'la petite fille japonaise aux cheveux noirs'* (he had taken French 'A' level). We took 'la petite fille' for breakfast at a café outside the Gare du Nord.

'You nice boys,' she said.

'Yes,' we replied, 'we're nice boys,' and for a couple of hours we splashed around happily in big cups of *café au lait*.

After breakfast we dumped our stuff at Mitzki's apartment and went to Père Lachaise to visit Baudelaire's grave. Leon and Charlie were interested in stuff like that then. Now they say things to me like 'Still doing books, Will?' – I write novels for the ten-to-fourteen market. It doesn't matter, they can't offend me. We're all bonded at the hip by childhood, and adolescent adventure, and by Annette.

We stood by the grave. It was covered in bouquets tossed by poetry lovers from all over the globe. An old man was sweeping the path nearby. 'Why should he get all the flowers?' he mumbled as he passed. 'I'm alive and I get shit.' Leon took out his notebook and wrote this down. He needed material for his daily postcard to Annette.

Mitzki let us sleep on the floor of her apartment for a week. It was torture. Every night she made love with her 'boyfriend', a married man who had sent his family south for the summer. He liked to show us pictures of his wife and kids, smiling on a pebbly Nice beach in front of the Hôtel Negresco. Then he'd get into bed with Mitzki and the two of them would pant and squeal and throw the covers off.

Charlie slept with his Swiss army knife open under the folded hood of his sleeping bag. Why did we stay? It was one of those crazy situations that you get into when you're eighteen and keep misreading everybody's motives and intentions. We thought Mitzki wanted to sleep with one of us, when in fact all she was after was an opportunity to express her gratitude for our ferry behaviour, and a little lively company during the long daytimes of zero contact with her lover.

After sex, when all animals are supposed to be silent and sad, Mitzki and Didier lay next to each other and whispered endearments in English, their chosen language of love. One night Mitzki said, 'I love to feel your winkle in me.' This was too much for Charlie. He jumped up, waving the knife, screaming, 'Shut up! It's not a winkle. It's not a fucking winkle.' Didier walked naked over to his attaché case and took out a small handgun.

We wandered all night around the Latin Quarter, and wound up in Montparnasse at a zinc bar on the Boulevard

Edgar-Quinet. On a wall nearby the entrance someone had spray-painted 'Choose Life'.

Every day Leon sent his postcard to Annette. He took a long time finding the appropriate reproduction or photograph, then he'd search out a perfect spot from which to write: a park bench in the Tuileries or a café on the Boul' Mich'.

Charlie said, 'Why don't you write all the cards together and then post them on different days?'

'It's not a chore, Charles,' Leon replied, 'I want to do it. Don't you understand? I love her.' Leon used to show me what he had written, tight, condensed little paragraphs full of intelligent reflection and considerate opinion. So that's love, I thought: taking the time, giving your best thoughts.

On our last night Charlie and I stayed up talking after Leon had gone to bed (we were now in a hotel on the Rue Delambre behind La Coupole). We got round to Annette, her great intensity of being, the way she threw herself into relationships as if they were life's great dramas (which they are).

'What a girl!' said Charlie.

'Yes,' I said, 'I feel anaemic when I'm in her company.'

Did I desire Annette? I had never let myself think so. Charlie clearly had aspirations in her direction, but I was the quiet, stand-at-the-back member of the group. I saw myself as a Nick Carraway type (I *was* reading Fitzgerald that summer), observing the extravagant actions of my friends with a mixture of wonder and detachment. 'By the way,' I said to Charles at the close of our long hymn to Annette – dawn was breaking through the window of our hotel room, a thick band of rose over a line of gold – 'what did you give her that day at the station?' Charlie gave me a blank look.

Two months after we returned from France, Leon and Annette got married. Everybody said the usual stuff to them, about how they were babies and ruining their lives.

They didn't care. 'We're going to live a Bohemian life,' Annette told Andrea Toker, Leon's mother. Leon, at this time, was planning a dual career as saxophonist and documentary film-maker.

'How exciting,' replied Mrs Toker. 'Do be sure to bathe from time to time.'

Getting married *was* unusual. No one from our generation seemed to be doing it then. It seemed like such a terrible curtailment of newly-won freedoms. In that ten-year footnote to history, 1965 to 1975, sans herpes, sans AIDS, sans everything, most of us thought life would go on forever as one happy tournament of torrid affairs and electrifying betrayals.

The wedding was a low-key affair, because they were babies. I was the best man. In those days, I carried an aura of responsibility in parental circles, a glow that faded over the years as Leon and Charlie went on to make much more money than me in the grown-up world of computers. Mrs Toker took over the proceedings from Annette's family who were 'poor as field mice'. She even dragged in Leon's father, a man whose name had been abomination in the Toker household for as long as anyone could remember.

'But what does Dad do?' asked Leon in the week before the wedding.

'He lies to people,' replied his mother.

In the end, Mrs Toker enjoyed herself. She spruced up the Highgate home, called in caterers, and arranged for a small canopy to be set up in the back garden. Annette got married in a low-cut white dress with matching mantilla. She looked like a killer señorita (I heard Mrs Toker mutter 'Portobello Road').

'You are about to wade down a long river,' said the rabbi, 'and, while your feet will get wet, you must learn to keep your heads above the water.' Leon smashed the glass, and we all cheered.

At the reception, Charlie got very stoned. This was

unfortunate as he had volunteered his services as photographer. Naturally, he only took 'candid' shots, but even these came out blurred. The only successes were twelve 'art' shots of an obscure Toker relative who weighed close to twenty stone.

'Did you ever see less tie in your life?' asked Charlie as he spread out the prints. 'Look at those trousers! They're up to his neck!' Mrs Toker never forgave him.

There's one other surviving picture (it wasn't taken by Charlie) showing the four of us grand revellers: Annette in between Charlie and Leon, and me leaning on Charlie's shoulder. Leon's got a distracted look on his face, his white shirt is creased and his glasses are misted up. I'm looking at Annette and Charlie, who are staring at each other. Charles is squeezing Annette's hand. Annette's got this fierce look in her eyes.

What does all this have to do with the current situation? Everything, because Annette is trying to hold Charlie to a twenty-four-year-old promise. It's 1992, and she wants Charlie to take her to Paris for a week. No big deal, right? Charlie's only her husband's lifelong best friend and business partner of fifteen years. Charlie's married too, by the way, to a barrister who wears designer clothes and takes home some scary salary. So you can see that there are all kinds of reasons why Charlie wouldn't gamble everything on opening out his marriage.

What has come over Annette? What made her rush into Charlie's office last month and wave the note that she had found while going through an old box of letters in her loft? Charlie rang Leon in the next office. 'Your wife's gone mad,' he said. 'She wants me to take her to Paris. Doesn't she have kids to look after?' Even as he was making this last remark, Charlie felt that it was a terribly old-fashioned thing for him to be saying. Nevertheless.

Leon promised to talk to Annette, but he only got a lecture. 'You went to Paris. You bastards. You didn't take me. You had a wonderful time. You wrote all about it. You all fucked some Japanese girl.' (Leon tried to interpose, but decided not to bother.) 'Charlie promised to take me next time. He wrote it in a note. "Next time, just you and me." He gave it to me at the station. I want him to keep his promise. Left Bank, wine, cheap hotel. I want the whole thing, Leon. I could have done it before our marriage, but I didn't.'

'Why not?' asked Leon.

'Because I loved you more,' Annette replied.

'Well, how about if I take you?'

'It won't be the same.'

'You can say that again,' said Leon.

'It's not even the sex,' Annette continued. 'I want *to be* in Paris, with Charlie.'

'But Charlie is not who he was. And in any case, he can't just take off for a week with you. What about his wife? What about work? What about me? I don't understand, Annette. You're a stable person.'

'A promise,' Annette replied, 'is a promise.'

The next day I got a conference call from Charlie and Leon. Annette seemed to be having an adolescent problem, and I was the specialist. But when I heard the story, I felt for Annette. I had just survived a marriage that had run aground on chores and arguments, and the drudgery of the quotidian. Oh, as bad for her as for me, but with no kids to keep us together, and enough money in the bank to keep both parties from impoverishment, we'd decided to call it a day. Still, the marriage *was* a failure, and I really hadn't wanted it to be. Perhaps if we'd been a little more accommodating of each other's illusions – I thought I could write a big novel for grown-ups without making any money while I was doing so, Laura thought she could have a child at forty-two – we might have stuck it out. Meanwhile eight years had passed. I knew all about lost chances.

So I understood Annette's desire to hold tight to the

promises of the past. Her great yearning to fit a missing piece back into the puzzle of her life, to take what had been denied her or what she had denied herself, and in doing so *not to pay a price* (can there be guilt when everything is out in the open?) for disrupting the lives of those she loved best. The children, by the way, would not be a problem. They were away at university and would know nothing of their mother's planned indiscretion.

But Leon and Charlie didn't see it this way. The computer champs thought it was all too silly for words. Charlie was a bit embarrassed, Leon a bit hurt, but really they were too distracted, by money and business, to give Annette's crazy idea more than a few days of their time. But she persisted, calling and harassing Charlie, until at last he told Leon, sadly, that he would have to call his lawyer.

Now here comes the beautiful part. Tomorrow, Annette and I leave for Paris. In the face of her determination and the discomfort of the legal arrangements, Charlie and Leon came up with yours truly as a compromise candidate, and, miracle of miracles, Annette agreed. Why do they (or Leon anyway) trust me? No one has mentioned sex, but the assumption seems to have been made that we will stay in separate rooms. Annette will get her week of freedom with good old, naïve old, Will, and then she will return to London; all signs of life replaced by signs of wife.

It's hard for me to tell this next part, because I haven't yet recovered. And maybe I won't. The taut guidelines by which I used to run my life – tolerance, acceptance, genuflexion to the forces of fate – have slackened. It may turn out that I am a bigger fool than my computer pals have imagined. On the other hand, for the first time that I can remember, I am wearing the stiff armour of commitment.

The first couple of days in Paris were fine. We took

separate rooms in the Hôtel des Grandes Écoles, the same place where the three *caballeros* had spent a night, after nearly being shot, back in 1968. In the mornings Annette and I met for breakfast and made plans. She had brought with her an offbeat guidebook, purchased shortly before we left, recommending tours of the sewers and that kind of thing. We opted for above ground, and searched out the little park on the banks of the Canal St-Martin. We sat on the bottom steps of a metal foot bridge, and watched the barges pass through the locks. At dusk, we wandered through the gardens in the Place des Vosges: fountains splashed, children played, old women in plastic folding chairs sat knitting and chatting. All this time we too talked happily, about the past, the present, the collapse of the Soviet Empire, the films we had seen recently, and so on.

On the second day, in the flea market on the Rue Jacob, Annette found a rose-patterned china plate that she liked. It had 'Made in England' stamped on the underside, but Annette was happy *simply to be buying something in Paris*. That evening we dined out in a bistro on the Left Bank. By mid-meal, we were deep into one of those rare conversations where every word spoken, including 'Could you pass the oil and vinegar?', seems significant and profound. When we returned to the hotel, Annette said, 'Well, this certainly beat a night at home with Leon and a video.' I shivered with guilt.

On the third night, after yet another great Parisian meal and a bottle and a half of *vin ordinaire*, we went back to the hotel and made love. We didn't plan it, it just sort of happened. 'It', by the way, was pretty good. Not the thrill of a lifetime, for either of us, but perfectly acceptable high-scoring sex, with a lot of general gratification all round. Now what? Should we do it again or forget about it? Would the guilt be the same from two nights as from one? Was one night forgivable spontaneity, and two nights systematic adultery? How could we look Leon in the face

when we got back? Was I a substitute for a fantasy of
Charlie? If so, how did I feel about being used? Alternat-
ively, and astonishingly, the possibility existed, it seemed
to me, that we were falling in love.

Lying in bed in the morning I searched the plots of my
teen-novels for a solution to our dilemma. From my books
a teenager could learn how to deal with all kinds of
emotional trials: divorced parents, loneliness at home and
at school, ineptitude in sports, awkwardness with members of the opposite sex. Somewhere, I usually threw in
a mystery or an adventure: Who was the old man in
the hut behind the rubbish dump whom Damien had
befriended? What did he know about Damien's father's
past? Or: Would the children, travelling in a gang, Billy
in the lead and Muffet the dog not far behind, make it
back from their extraordinary excursion across the wilder-
ness that lay beyond the farm?

No luck. Nothing in my imaginative life had prepared
me for the mystery and adventure of that Paris morning:
the sight of Annette's half-naked body, stretch marks
plainly visible on her full breasts; the watery light that
filtered through the hotel windows and fell in shafts on
her pale English face.

Annette woke and the first thing she said was, 'Well,
there's not much point carrying on paying for two rooms,
is there?' As soon as she spoke, and I heard the matter-
of-fact tone in her voice, I knew that I had misread the
situation. Annette had an agenda, sex was on it, that was
all. If I did something stupid, like fall in love with her
(and I already felt that I was on the verge), I would ruin
her plans. I was neither a stand-in for Charlie, nor a
replacement for Leon. I was simply part of the package
tour. The fact that *I* was chosen and not some strange
guy off a dance floor wasn't negligible, it made everything
cosier, less risky, and Annette really couldn't be resented,
in our sexually fraught decade, for wanting to err on the
side of security.

Once I understood that she was running her own show, I said, 'Tell me something, did Charlie really write "next time just you and me" in that note? It sounds so pat and clichéd, not like him at all.'

'The note?' Annette responded, doing up her bra at the front (why didn't they ever think of that before?).

'The one you found in your attic?'

'Oh, I didn't find any note,' she continued nonchalantly, 'I made that up.'

'You're kidding.' I sat up dumbfounded in the bed. 'But I saw you. At Victoria Station, I saw him hand you a note.'

'Well, yes, that's true, he did,' she replied, 'but I didn't find it, I sort of remembered it, and then I rewrote it. It was a love letter, but I couldn't swear that he promised to take me to Paris. It seems he didn't remember the contents either.'

I whispered, 'Nice work,' under my breath, and then, louder, 'I'm impressed.'

'Women have to move the goalposts.' She was wriggling into her skirt with a kind of slalom motion. 'We have to play with the rules. Because you made up the rules.'

'So there was no promise.'

'Isn't there always a promise in youth?' Annette replied, giving me a big smile. She was now fully dressed. 'Let's do a museum for a change,' she said and with both hands pulled me up out of the bed.

In the Musée d'Orsay, we paused in front of Monet's painting of the interior of the Gare St-Lazare. Annette read to me out of the guidebook, something Zola once said about how artists must find the poetry of the railway station just as their fathers found that of the woods and rivers. Suddenly, I felt hot and sweaty. Was I going to faint? Annette put her cool hands on my brow. Out of the painting, clouds of steam and blue-white smoke rolled under the broad sheds, and enveloped me. I had not had an experience like this for a very long time, and then it had been chemically induced. I interpreted the hallucination quite simply, and stupidly, as *the magic of love*.

Over lunch, in the museum cafeteria, in that long space of Parisian time (it is, after all, a city given over to appetite) between the salad and the coffee, I poured out my heart. 'I've fallen in love with you,' I said, and followed up with a strong series of embarrassing clichés. I definitely said, 'I think I have loved you since I first met you,' and I may, at some point, have quoted a Marvin Gaye song. Annette was very understanding, and, so she said, 'flattered'. She also didn't laugh, which was nice. However, she was not going to let me turn her world upside-down.

'It's a one-off, Will. I needed a break, I *really* needed a break. But I'm not terribly unhappy. I've loved being with you this week. You were a great companion, and the sex was good, but we have to stop now.'

So that was it. Good old, naïve old, Will, fell hard. He couldn't accept a small gift without wanting more. Was I greedy? And what about Annette? How could she go back to cleaning the house, doing the shopping, and making the dinners, when everything was unalterably changed? After all, a painting had come to life. Except that for her, it hadn't. All she had wanted was a week, not a miracle. She'd had her week.

Back in London, Charlie, and more importantly, Leon, hardly seemed to have noticed that we'd been away. In our absence, their computer company, which markets programs to firms of accountants, had snared a fat new client in the City. Charlie and Leon had spent the week in what they liked to call 'intense negotiations'. They had come out with a sale. When Leon picked us up at the airport he was in high spirits, jubilant.

Since then, the question that I have kept asking myself is: 'Did it mean something or nothing?' Taking the latter proposition first: my friends and I were men and women in their forties living in the poisonous West; what did we have to look forward to except lumps in our testicles or breasts, or surgeons cleaving at our chest bones to get at our plaque-filled arteries? So what did it matter if a couple of grown-ups of the species took a week in Paris to fool around with each other's bodies? On the other hand, if it didn't matter at all, wasn't that bigger trouble? Wasn't love the thin membrane on which the whole weighty culture trembled and shook? Oh, I wished I was a Masai, standing tall and straight with my attack-resistant heart beating under a clear African sky. Surely, there was a place, perhaps in the highlands of Tanzania, where confusion was banished.

Two months have passed. Last week Charlie rescinded his restraining order. He'd kept it up all this time in case Annette 'went loopy' again, but so far the only person losing their mind is me.

One night recently I slept in my car outside Leon and Annette's house in Muswell Hill. It rained all night, and when I awoke, damp and chilled, it was still coming down in that grey London drizzle that dulls the spirit and depresses the heart. When, around 10 am, Annette came out and got in her car, I followed her. She parked at the supermarket.

'What's this? Fatal Attraction?' she said when she saw me, unkempt and unshaven, coming down the aisle. She was wearing a long purple coat, and had her hair bunched up on the top of her head. In front of her was a trolley top-heavy with toilet paper and washing powder.

We stood next to the tinned tomatoes while I tried to convince her to change her life. I told her why I thought we'd be the perfect couple, why Leon wouldn't be hurt, why she was so wonderful. When I finished Annette said, 'You're projecting.' I *hated* that word. Nobody was ever in love any more, all they did was 'project' and 'transfer'.

· 'It must be possible to go beyond terminology,' I said, 'to be star-crossed, fated, born for each other.'

By the end of our conversation I thought I'd convinced Annette at least to give me another hearing. But when and where? It was left vague.

Yesterday, we all had dinner together in a Chinese restaurant: Leon, Annette, Charlie, his wife, and a friend of Charlie's wife, another woman lawyer, an attractive, clever person who was supposed to be a set-up for me. There was a lot of talking and joking about the Paris trip. Charlie, in particular, acted as if Annette and I had just got back from scout and guide camp, Leon was a little more subdued, but not much. 'Well, I think it's wonderful,' said Kyla, the woman lawyer, 'that two friends of the opposite sex can do a thing like that. Why not? It should happen more often. Men and women, married men and women, are so scared of each other. I have male friends, some from as far back as school – they can't even have lunch with me without feeling guilty. They call their wives at the beginning and the end of the meals. They tell them every course. I even hear them describing our conversations; they make them sound like the most tepid exchanges the world has ever known.'

So there we were, Annette and I, champions of the platonic life, exemplary friends, and all I could see in my mind was that broad bed in the hotel, with its Swiss roll bolster, the exemplary friends caressing each other's middle-aged bodies, thinking about nothing except what to do next that might give more pleasure to the other person.

At the end of the meal, after we had drunk our coffee and were waiting for the bill, I felt someone's foot pressing something against mine. I looked down: it was a paper napkin. I picked it up surreptitiously. The note said 'Let's meet again.' I looked over at Annette, thinking how beautiful and brilliant of her, how symmetrical and perfect, how adventurous and sexy. But Annette was deep in conversation with Charlie's wife, discussing how to ensure that their children used condoms. Kyla, her eyes shining, smiled nervously at me.

Charcoal on Paper

My old girlfriend Hermine David once said, 'You can do anything you like with me.' We were in the heat of passion on a rooftop mattress on New York's Upper West Side. I don't know why, but I took a plum from a bowl that we'd brought up with us and ate it from between her thighs. What a confusion of mouths and juices! I remembered this moment last spring – not that I'd ever really forgotten it – when I was standing in front of three erotic drawings by Pascin, one of which showed a couple naked and embracing in a bare room with only a bowl of fruit for company.

I was in a small gallery in the village of Ein Kerem, near Jerusalem. I had been travelling on museum business and a friend had tipped me off to the Pascins. They were for sale at a high price, but reasonably high, and I thought it would be a coup for the little museum that I run in New York if I could bring them back.

To tell the truth I wanted to impress the trustees. I'd been in trouble ever since the sheep and I needed to reestablish myself. I should have known that a conceptual artist herding twenty sheep, each stencilled with Stars of David and the Palestinian flag, into three rooms on the Upper East Side wouldn't go down well, but I'd figured that what was good enough for the Venice Biennale should have been good enough for the Little Museum of Jewish Art. 'Let's get back to taste,' Ross and Krentzman said to me at our Monday-morning meeting (the philistines), 'charcoal on paper, something like that.' They packed me off to Israel to buy anything I could find that was art but inoffensive.

Anyway, there I was in this low-ceilinged white room checking out the Pascins and thinking about Hermine when who should come in but Hermine! 'Julius!' she said. 'My God, what are you doing here?' She looked as pleased to see me as I was shocked to see her, doubly shocked because as soon as she spoke I saw that it wasn't Hermine but her little sister Erith who had been fourteen, furtive, and angry the last time I had seen her, more than ten years ago.

We went and sat in a nearby garden café and held hands in silence for a while as if the two of us really had been the lovers. Butterflies fluttered around our heads and a waiter with an old-fashioned stomach (the kind that hangs over the trouser belt – you simply don't see them in New York any more) brought our coffee. Erith told me her story. She had been borne over to Israel on the tiny, crestless wave of emigration from Upper Manhattan that followed the Yom Kippur War. She had met a painter and married him. With money borrowed from her father (did I remember that corrupt individual and his fraudulent business practices?), she had opened this gallery. She didn't show her husband's work – he was for other markets – but they both made money and she lived well. I asked about Hermine. Erith told me that she taught EFL at the College of the Desert in California. She lived alone.

All the time that Erith was talking, I was stoking up twin lusts. The first was for Hermine. I had visions of the old mattress and then, better still, the water bed where she and I had sunk and squelched through three years of Columbia grad school. Every time Erith bent forward to pick up her coffee cup her loose white blouse would expose her cleavage and I'd have this rush of memory, Hermine sitting astride me, her breasts hanging pendulously over my face. But I was also after the Pascins and, in my mind, I had already begun wheeler-dealing, wondering how I could use the 'old friends' angle to lower the price.

'Come and meet Albert,' said Erith, 'he's working in his studio.'

'Love to,' I said. I was thinking, 'Redemption.' 'Salvation.'

Albert was standing, brush in hand, at the far end of a large shed which we entered through a door at the back of the gallery. When he saw us he ran to grab a tarpaulin and draped it over the canvas he was working on. Looking around I couldn't fathom what he was being so sensitive about. His studio was full of the worst kitsch: sunsets in Jerusalem, sunsets in Safed, the Hebrew alphabet in bright colours, Wailing Wall scenes, bearded *tzaddiks*, all done with a thick palette knife. Albert waved his hand. 'For the Americans,' he said. He moved around in a small circle covering various other works in progress. All artists, no matter how bad, have their pride I guess. Albert was entitled to his creative privacy if he wanted it.

Albert walked over to us and I noticed that one leg dragged slightly. Erith introduced us. We did the coincidence and mistaken identity stuff. Albert gave me a long stare, shook my hand, then slapped me hard on the back, kibbutz-style. Erith said, 'Stay for lunch,' and I said, no, I had to be getting back to the hotel.

Then, as I was going out the front door, I turned into Mr Nonchalance and said, 'Oh, I see you have Pascins.'

'Yes, aren't they wonderful?' said Erith. I thought for a moment. 'He's a great draughtsman but there's a soft-porn aspect to his work, sometimes he's almost, you know, kitsch.' I didn't want to leave her with the impression that I wasn't at all interested, so I added, 'But I'd like to take another look at them.'

'Come tomorrow night, for dinner, some people are coming over.'

'I will,' I said. 'It's good to see you Erith.'

'You too Julius, you were kind to me when I was a teen.'

I was glad to hear this information about myself. Kindness wasn't a virtue that I had practised much in adult life, and now that I knew that I'd been kind in the past it made it easier to be cruel in the present. I was going to rip Erith off – it would balance the relationship.

I went back to the La Romme and searched for my wife (haven't I mentioned her?) down by the pool. I've been married a long time, Lucy was even around in the time of Hermine. In fact, for a while I was torn between them. Hermine was passionate and loving and super-smart but she had an overbearing mother always dragging the good daughter off to cater to her needs. During one of these absences I took up with Lucy, whom I'd describe as 'fore-shortened' – in all areas: emotional range, intelligence, height. At first I thought of these attributes as pleasing little-girl qualities and it was a turn-on. But I soon knew that I'd sabotaged myself for the sake of some companion-ship and extra sex. So why did I marry her? These things aren't easy. Hermine dumped me soon after the sixties kicked in. Her parting words were, 'Deep down you're a shallow man, Julius.' I was left with an ABD in Art History and a Lucy who was willing to type my thesis. Up in her room Lucy had a collection of MOMA reproduction fertility gods. She'd type, I'd flick through art books and watch TV, then the statues would start to go to work.

'Mr Pincas,' the doorman said when I came up from the pool, 'your wife left a message for you. She's gone to the Islamic Clock Museum, she'll be back later tonight.'

I went up to our room, lay on the bed, and stared at the painting (probably done by Albert) of a half-dressed Bathsheba washing at the well. What was currently erotic in my life? Nothing! Those pre-Columbian figures weren't doing it for me any more. I looked at Bathsheba. Nothing. Suddenly the figure in the painting spoke to me. She used the voice of my Uncle Leon who had once said to me, 'Your mother thinks your hair is made of mink.'

'What do you want from me?' said Bathsheba. 'Jews don't do erotics, they do Torah plates and matza covers.

If you want slits and members and servants tittering in the corner, you'll have to look somewhere else.'

'Okay,' I said to Bathsheba/Leon, 'what about Pascin? The heaviness of the women's bodies, the unconventional perspective so it feels as if you're standing over one woman or sitting very close to another who has her legs casually parted. What about that?'

The phone rang. It was Krentzman from New York. 'Any luck?' he said.

'I'm close to something.'

'Is it on canvas or livestock?'

'I can't hear you,' I yelled. 'The line, there's interference . . .' and I put the phone down.

The following night we took a cab to Ein Kerem. Lucy brought along her collection of postcards from the clock museum to show me on the way – I'd been too tired to look the night before. As soon as we began the winding descent to the village Lucy said, 'This reminds me of parts of Italy.' She was always being reminded of somewhere we weren't. The cypresses and pines stood straight up against the darkening sky, terraced olives swirled in gnarled contours, and the open windows of the cab let in the lightest of scents, honeysuckle – or was it jasmine? It was the kind of night I thought I deserved for being such a mild-mannered guy who did no harm to the world.

The party was on the roof, which itself had a kind of trellised roof draped with vines and hung with dried herbs. The guests were art collectors, other gallery owners, a couple of poets. Next to me sat Mildred Teppish, a woman now in her seventies who had spent most of her life driving around the south of France, visiting studios and buying art. Everyone had heard of the Teppish collection: museum curators humbled themselves when she came into town. On my other side was curly-haired, handsome Albert, who, as the evening progressed, turned out to be the last of the old-style *raconteurs*. Albert's subject was family: his three fat lipsticked

sisters and his parents, all crowded in the Tunisian moon-
light of memory on their waterfront home. What a long-
suffering woman Bertha Ben Simon had been! After the
children had grown up and left, Albert's father, seizing
the opportunity, had packed his bags too. Bertha took to
her kitchen, boiled water in pots and, for the benefit of
the neighbours, carried on loud conversations with an
imaginary husband. At this point of the story Albert cried.

I wanted to steer the conversation to the Pascins but
Mrs Teppish took the wheel.

'How on earth did you get those sexy drawings, Erith?'

'Ask Albert,' Erith said laconically.

Mrs Teppish turned eagerly towards him. I realized that
I had a big-money rival. Albert began, not with the history
of his acquisition, but with the story of Pascin. He told
us of the artist's long, boring childhood after the family
had moved from Bulgaria to Bucharest, and the even
longer hours in his father's grain business. He told us of
Pascin's dream of a free life completely devoted to art and
how it was achieved in Paris in the years after 1905 when
the painter behaved like an oriental prince and trailed a
party of fifty in ten taxis from Montmartre to Montparnasse. He described the years in America, Pascin's fas-
cination with the South, his watercolours of Negro jazz
musicians in New Orleans, his trips to Cuba, the house
that he bought in Charleston, South Carolina. He told of
the return to Paris, the exhaustion, the suicidal
depressions, and, tragically, the suicide itself, the slit
wrists, the note to his lover written in blood on the walls
of his studio. 'Forgive me.'

Albert stopped, as if he were waiting for a chill to creep
into the night air. I felt a movement behind my back and
turned around. A fig tree pressed its leaves on the roof's
side trellis like a child pressing hands on a windowpane.
Only Mrs Teppish remained unabsorbed into the world
of the artist; not for her the painter hanging from a peg
on his door, the floor strewn with cigarette butts, works

piled up all over. 'But where did you get the drawings?' she insisted, and her voice was the tinny ring of a till opening and closing.

'Ah, that's another story,' said Albert, and he dipped his pitta into a bowl of babaganoush.

On the way home Lucy stretched out her legs and just failed to touch the back of the driver's seat. 'That Albert was such a phoney,' she said. 'I think he was putting on an accent to go with those dark handsome looks.'

'Don't be ridiculous,' I replied, and I thought how typical of her to be unable to respond when someone was talking about things that mattered – passion, commitment, wildness, and death.

Sunday morning, first thing, I went back to the gallery which had been closed for the Sabbath. Erith was alone, sponging the tiled floor of the two white rooms. I stood in the doorway and looked across to the Pascins. One of them had a square of paper stuck on the wall next to it. I strained my eyes but couldn't make out what was written. I would have to wait for the floor to dry to get close. Erith backed out of the second room and said, 'I'll go and make coffee, come up when you're ready, Julius.'

I took off my shoes and stepped across the wet tiles, warm water soaking through the bottom of my socks. The sign, handwritten in elegant script, said, 'On Loan from the Collection of Mrs Mildred Teppish.' I couldn't believe it. I stood holding my shoes in my hands, staring back and forth from the label to the drawing, where a woman lay on her side on a bed, her nightdress pushed up to her waist, a dark inviting charcoal smear exposed to the man who crouched on all fours over her.

'Something the matter, Julius?' said a voice behind me. I kept my silence. 'You let out a little cry.'

'I did? Well, I'm surprised. Mrs Teppish. How could she? When? I mean . . .'

Erith beckoned from the doorway. 'Come up and I'll tell you about it.'

I followed her upstairs to the roof and saw clearly for the first time that, in body anyway, she was not like her sister at all.

Mrs Teppish, it turned out, had driven away from their house on Friday night only to return in the early hours of Saturday morning – she had tried to get to sleep but couldn't, she had to buy a Pascin, probably all of them, but one would do for now. She offered an enormous amount of money – eighty thousand dollars – more than twice what they were hoping to get for the drawing. They accepted with delight. And why was the drawing still in the gallery? Mrs Teppish wanted a different frame and Albert was going to change it for her.

I wanted to say, 'I'll take the others,' but Mrs T. had raised the stakes considerably and I was in danger of breaking the Little Museum's budget. Ross and Krentzman wouldn't be pleased. To give myself some breathing space I changed the subject. We chatted and took in the pleasant early summer air and stared down off the roof into a neighbouring garden where an old woman was feeding a couple of scrawny chickens. It sounded as if she had the radio on, for some exquisite music was drifting around her and up to us.

'What's that music?' I said.

'It's the choir practising,' Erith replied, and she waved across the village to a building high up in the hills. 'There's a convent there, a few old Russian nuns, they're all in their seventies and eighties, they can't sing the liturgy any more so they've taken local girls from the village and trained them. They've got Arab girls singing in Old Slavonic – haunting, isn't it?'

We listened intently for a while, the chickens scrabbled around in the old woman's yard while on another, lower rooftop, a mother and small son had appeared. They'd made a line of pots out of abandoned sinks and now they were filling them with soil.

'Look Erith,' I said, 'I'll be straight with you. I'm in

trouble at home. I've had a disaster. I met this crazy Israeli at a party, Zalman Kevesh, he does this conceptual stuff with sheep. He snowed me, talked with amazing confidence, very intense. Big guy with a beard. You know the way it can be. I gave him a show. No need to go into details but it all backfired. I need the Pascins and I'll give you eighty thousand for the two that are left. I can't go any higher.' I didn't want to mention the kindnesses that I'd performed towards her in her lonely teen years – she'd told me that I'd bought her her first camera – but I was hoping that the pulls and tugs of the past would jerk things in my favour.

Erith thought a while then said, 'Julius, I want to do it, but you'll have to talk to Albert.'

Albert was driving to Safed to take his works to a gallery that catered to the tourist trade. He invited me to come along with him and although it was close to a three-hour drive I figured that I had to accept. Between Jerusalem and Tel Aviv he repeated the Friday-night stories about growing up in Tunis. Between Tel Aviv and Haifa (we dropped off three rabbis blowing ram's horns and two Jerusalem sunsets at a Tel Aviv gallery), Albert described his life in Paris. He had arrived penniless in 1959. After a series of menial jobs he had met Vidil Moses. This woman, Pascin's last mistress, was close to sixty. Albert became her driver and shopper, then personal assistant, and finally he had become her lover, yes, her lover! It was Vidil who had encouraged him to paint and, timidly at first, but then with increasing confidence and skill, he had become Albert the artist, filling their apartment off the Avenue Foche with colourful works that Vidil's friends wickedly described as belonging to the 'Infantile' school of art. But Albert knew the paintings were true as his heart.

From Haifa to Safed I learned that after Vidil's death, Albert, friendless in Paris and short on cash, had come to Israel and remade himself as an Israeli artist specializing in biblical scenes (Jacob and the mess of pottage was his favourite). Again people scoffed, but Albert had confidence in himself and expected to make money. He didn't. Two wars came and went, Albert got a bullet in the ankle. Times were hard. Then, like magic, on his fiftieth birthday good luck came Albert's way. A French official called him from Paris; a codicil to Vidil's will had been discovered. She had bequeathed him the three Pascins!

By now we were in Safed and walking up the last steps of a narrow stone stairway. We had come around to the back of the gallery. Albert pushed open a door into a room crowded with canvases. I put down the two paintings that he had given me to carry.

'The Pascins,' I said. 'Will you sell them to me?'

'You want all three,' he said. 'I can't do it.'

'I know,' I said. 'I understand that Mrs Teppish has already bought one.'

'That's right.' Albert looked at me with his beautiful open face and began to smile. 'But I like you Julius,' he said. 'And in a way we are like brothers – you and Erith's sister, Erith and me.' He made a small circle with his thumb and forefinger and slowly pushed a finger of his other hand back and forth through the hole. It was a vulgarity that I somehow hadn't expected from him. He asked me if I'd buy all three drawings if I could and I said, 'Yes, but I can't match Mrs Teppish's prices and anyway . . .'

Albert interrupted me. 'She hasn't paid anything yet; nothing is signed. But tell me, Julius, why should I lose forty thousand dollars, even if you are my brother-in-love.'

Well, he had me there, but on the other hand I sensed that he *wanted* to sell the drawings to me and this I understood perfectly well. We all have these impulses and sometimes we'll take a financial loss for the unqualified good feeling that the other transaction gives us. Mrs Teppish was horrible. I'd seen her in action. And who would see the drawings? Only Mrs Teppish and her rich friends. At the Little Museum thousands would wander by and be thrilled.

Okay, Albert, I thought. Good man. You want to go where your feelings are taking you, and it's not a mistake. You'll still wind up over six figures.

Albert must have been reading my thoughts. 'I'll sell you the Teppish drawing for sixty thousand and the others at your original offer.'

'Done,' I said. 'Ross and Krentzman can come up with another twenty grand. Let them take it out of their JNF contributions to Israel.'

'Tell them my name is Israel,' said Albert and we shook hands.

On the way back to Jerusalem Albert was surprisingly silent. We came down the fast way, through Tiberias, and stopped there for a late lunch. We sat in a restaurant overlooking the Kinneret and ate St Peter's fish. Albert was almost glum.

'What's the matter?' I said. 'You've just made a lot of money.'

'Yes,' he said, 'but it's still hard to part with them.'

'I understand this,' I replied, my heart beating fast. 'It's a sort of post-coital *tristesse* undergone by artists and owners alike. I imagine you know it from both sides. Writers don't have the same problem; they write something and they can reproduce it as many times as they want. Words are easily translatable, into books, onto photocopying paper, down fax machines. But for a painter it's *einmal* only. You know Kundera? *Einmal ist keinmal.* You sell your work, you never see it again. Same for a collector, you sell it, it's gone. It's the pain of the potty, that first recognition that something you've made is flushing away. Nasty.'

Albert had been looking at me with increasing scepticism and I supposed that there was something about my babble that he found incompatible with the setting – tranquil lake, fishermen fixing nets. But then the expression on his face changed and he yelled, 'But what if what you have created stinks? My work stinks! You think I don't know that? I can part with that crap without shedding a tear. But the Pascins are special! The drawings are alive! Sometimes I imagine that I have slept with his women. They are my heart's darlings and my centrefolds. I never saw such. Hair! Breasts! Half dressed! Undressed! Rear views! Front views!'

I felt sorry for the guy. When we were back in the car I said, 'Are you sure you want to go ahead with this, Albert?' He looked straight ahead for a while but then slowly nodded his head in assent.

The next day I sent two cables to Ross and Krentzman. The first said, 'Dear Al and Leo. Go suck on shankbone.' This was a mental cable. The second, which I actually sent, said, 'Little Museum Makes Big Purchase: Pascins at Bargain Price.' Albert and I had set an official exchange time for late that night. I had to get a bank cheque and he had to draw up the documents of authenticity. So I found myself with a celebratory day off and as I was feeling good I acquiesced when Lucy said that she wanted to spend a day at the beach.

We took a *sherut* down to Tel Aviv. The seven passengers were five Hasidim and ourselves. None of them were allowed to touch Lucy so she got squeezed up between me and the door. All five chain-smoked and averted their eyes from my wife whose skirt slid up her thighs every time I shifted on the bench seat. Or did they avert? I thought I caught a few sneaks and even started to get the feeling that Lucy was enjoying herself.

Out near the Sheraton hotel we found a nice deserted beach but it turned out to be divided for religious purposes into male and female precincts. A hundred yards down the sand it was all bronzed flesh and brazen swimsuits. Lucy said she'd rather swim where it was quiet and I said, 'That's okay, but you'll have to stay without me.'

I wandered over to the crowded beach and found a spot to dump my stuff. It was noisy: radios were blaring, kids were playing paddleball. I walked down to the water: it was a sour, uninviting, urinous green, but I swam never-theless, bobbing the warm waves with a bunch of scream-ing ten-year-olds. I showered off the salt, then went and lay face down on my towel. The sounds of the beach and the crashing waves rolled over me.

A procession was coming towards me across the sand. It looked like a group of whores from some Jazz Age Paris bordello. They were all in frilly nightdresses with garishly painted faces. Tel Aviv's red light district was nearby on Hayarkon Street, but this looked like beach theatre. Two girls came and stood over me; from my supine perspective they loomed enormously large. One was squeezing her breasts and rolling her eyes in some horrible parody of a whore, the other looked distraught. In heavily accented English the sad one said, 'But how are we going to cut them back on?' I saw that the buttons of her nightdress were hanging by their threads.

'No, no,' I said. 'You mean *sew* them back on.'

She raised up her palms to me as if to say, 'What can I do?' Her hands were two bloody stumps severed at the wrists.

I must have slept for a while, long enough for the sun to have burned the back of my neck. I wrapped my shirt into a scarf, wetted it under a nearby fountain and wrapped it around my neck. I walked over to the empty religious beach (what a waste of seafront sand!) and found Lucy. While she was changing I told her my dream.

We went to eat at Zelig's on Ibn Gavirol Street. While we were waiting for our salads, I said, 'That dream has got something to do with the Pascins.'

Lucy was ready for me. 'Brilliant,' she said. 'You really picked something up in therapy.' Then she started in about my narcissism and vanity. 'You don't think of

anyone except yourself,' that kind of thing. For good measure she added, 'And you think you're such a stud.'

I took umbrage. 'I have to get my pleasures elsewhere
because I don't get them from you.'

'Look, Julius,' she said, 'don't get nasty just because I
don't want to play fruit salad with you.'

'How do you know about that?'

'You told me, of course, right after we met, practically
on the first date. You were stoned and trying to get me
into bed. I think you thought the story would turn me
on.'

'And did it?'

'Unlike Hermine I don't find plums stimulating access-
ories. I'd rather have something that's still attached to the
bough, that blooms while it fades, know what I mean?'

'Not exactly,' I said, but I did know that she was on a
roll and things were going badly for me. I tried catching
the waiter's eye. (Bring that food!)

'It's you, Julius,' I heard Lucy continue. 'You're the one
who's "not there". You look at paintings and drawings
all day, and all night you look at pictures in your head.'

'Everybody does that.'

'You don't see my body.'

'That's because you don't like to expose it.'

And we were off, sniping and wounding. She wouldn't
let up about that plum, so finally I yelled, 'It was erotic!
Erotic!'

And do you know what she said? 'Eros wasn't a Jewish
god.'

We got back to Jerusalem about six-thirty and I went
off to meet Albert. I waited at the Café Rondo for half an
hour. No one came. I had the bank cheque in my pocket
and I kept touching it to make sure that it hadn't disappeared. It was a warm evening and the place was almost
empty; most people were out strolling. The few of us who
were there sat outside on the terrace overlooking a small
park. In front of us, in a fenced-off garden area, two

municipal workers were struggling with a heavy sculpture, trying to set it in place on a plinth. They looked exhausted and had clearly been working for some time on what was more than a two-man job. The sculpture looked like an Arp, some kind of anthropomorphic female form. The workers tried to get a grip, they spread their arms around the stone curves, pressed their bodies to it and heaved. Nothing moved. They tried turning their backs, then one turned and put his arm through a lacuna and lifted, then they pushed and rocked and hugged. Finally, the sculpture shifted, but as it did so it momentarily trapped one of the workers' feet. He let out a yell that stopped the evening walkers in their tracks. Crushed by Art! *That's* why the Jews were suspicious of graven images: the Egyptians had crushed them with Art! Sculpture brought tribal nightmares to us all.

While all this was going on Erith had come onto the terrace and pulled up a chair next to mine. She was smiling.

'The drawings are in the car,' she said, 'but let me get some coffee.'

'Are you crazy?' I said. 'Let's get the art *now* and put it in security at the hotel. And where's Albert?' I asked. 'Didn't he want to come to collect the big prize?'

Erith shook her head. 'He's depressed. He went for a walk, said he was going up to the convent.'

'Not to join, I hope.' I was full of laughs, triumphant, benevolent, home free. I handed over the cheque.

Before going down to security I decided to take a quick look at my purchases. I went up to the room and laid the drawings out on the bed. There they were, the heavy women and the skimpy men, the bowl of fruit (apples). The lines were a little thicker than I had remembered them, the draughtsmanship less exquisite than I had first thought – but they were masterpieces nonetheless. More than that, they were masterpieces of Modern Jewish Art. Ross and Krentzman would be delighted. 'You're a

genius,' I said to myself, and then, with a nod at the
drawings, I added, 'You too, Pascin.'

But what about poor old Albert? I couldn't leave the
man down and out when he had turned out to be my
redeemer in Zion. I decided to pay him a visit and cheer
him up. I'd tell him some of the things that he could buy
with his money. Or, better still, I'd tell him what a fine
person he was for elevating himself above the material.

Down in the lobby I spotted Mrs Teppish. 'Hey, Milly,'
I shouted as she was crossing the floor. 'What's up in the
World of Art?' I closed on her, remembering only at the
last minute that I had better not gloat over my victory.
She didn't know it was the sweetness of my personality
that had lured Albert out of her clutches.

'Mr Pincas,' she said, fishing my name out of a dank
pond. 'The Pascins, did you buy them?'

I was taken aback and I wasn't quite sure what to say.
Well, what did it matter now?

'Yes,' I said. 'I bought them all.'

'I *knew* you would,' she said. 'You had that look in
your eyes, you know. You must be very interested in the
erotic.' I let this pass. 'Nowadays,' she went on, 'I prefer
work that's a little less exciting, if you get my point.' The
point? The point was that she was a bad loser pretending
that she hadn't given a damn anyway. Or was that the
point? In the taxi on the way to Ein Kerem I started to
think a little. By the time we stopped at Albert's place I
was in a fury of anticipation. I ran around the back of the
house to Albert's studio. It was locked. I picked up an
iron rod from a nearby heap of rubble – there are dumps
like this all over Jerusalem – and forced the door of
Albert's studio. The place was as before: a few paintings
leaned on the walls; a work in progress (rabbi with ram's
horn at sunset) was on the easel.

I walked over to Albert's painting table. It was covered
in squeezed paint tubes, scraps of rag and paper. A bouquet of brushes was set in a jar of turpentine. I started to

rummage through the stuff on the table. I threw a pile of old newspapers onto the floor. I knew, oh, I knew what I was looking for. And yes, yes, here, pressed flat under the heavy base of a desk lamp, were Albert's sketches, the heavy charcoal lines, the oh-so-familiar poses. But worse, much worse, each sketch had a photograph paper-clipped to its top left-hand corner. The pictures, slightly out of focus, looked as if they been taken with a kid's first camera; they showed Hermine and me on her water bed, rolling, grappling, panting, and, in the last one, screaming open-mouthed.

I sped down through the terraced olive groves, then up through a copse of fig trees. I could see the convent in the distance but I had no idea how to get to it. At the top of the hill, out of breath, I paused to rest by a tree. Some strange, globular, semi-translucent fruit hung from its branches. I put my hand out to touch one of them; it was sticky, not altogether pleasant.

Suddenly a voice, Albert's, but slurred and loud, came out of nowhere. 'Do you know what you are touching?' he said. 'The testicles of the leaders of the American Jewish community.' He laughed drunkenly. I crested the hill and saw him on a pinnacle thirty feet above me, from which vantage point he had spied me under the tree. He was sitting on a large rock to one side of the convent gate, a two-litre wine bottle cradled on his knees. I wanted to grab him by the throat but we were separated by a ravine twenty feet wide. Below us was a dizzying drop into what looked like a well on the outskirts of the village. For a moment it was silent, then the voices of the convent choir began to rise in praise and lament.

I started to speak but Albert was ahead of me. 'I put my heart into them,' he yelled. 'The rest doesn't matter.' He stood up from the rock and arched the wine bottle down into the ravine; it spun and curved a long time before hitting the ground. No sound reached us, but a group of small figures scattered and gesticulated. I took a step forward and almost lost my footing. The sun was sinking in a great flame behind Albert's back, the sky looked like one of his paintings come alive. 'Ross and Krentzman will kill you,' I shouted. It was pathetic.

Not Far from Jericho

Meyer accelerates past the yellowing, roofless walls of an abandoned refugee camp, a decaying honeycomb spread out on both sides of the road. He says, 'Look at it. Can you believe that? That's not us you know, we didn't build that. That's them, from '48.' Varda touches a finger to her lips then rubs at an imaginary mark on her white blouse.

'You shouldn't have come this way.'

'We're late, aren't we?'

'Even so.'

Ari, her nephew, is asleep in the back seat. Recently, he's undergone a growth spurt. His long legs have nowhere to go, his feet are pressed against one of the rear side windows of the Citroën.

'I think your sister would rather have us there on time.'

'My sister would rather have us there alive.'

'Don't be silly.'

They pass through two army road blocks: metal teeth set in the road, small wasteful flares, sentry boxes, each holding a young soldier cradling an M-16. At each checkpoint Meyer has to explain why they have come his way. No, they don't live in one of the settlements. Yes, they are on their way north, to a wedding. And they are *late*. The soldiers remonstrate with him. Why not go the other way? So he'd get to the wedding late? So what? Meyer says, 'I have a right to go any way I want, and *you're* supposed to make it safe for me to do so.'

Meyer leans forward and turns on the radio. He twists the dial, and comes up with a phone-in show. He doesn't want to listen to Hebrew, and tries to locate the English-language news. At first there is static, then the swirl and ripples of an Arabic song, short bursts of pipe and tabor, then deep, long-drawn-out wails and calls. Finally he picks up the station he wants. In Gaza three Palestinians have been shot, and a soldier killed by a cement block dropped on his head.

Varda says, 'Do we have to listen to this?'

Meyer rolls down the window. It is late winter in Jerusalem, chilly and damp, but here it feels like spring. There's a thick, pungent scent coming into the car. Somewhere nearby, orchards are in blossom, but you can't see them. His immediate superior at the bank once told him that Palestinian farmers still use human excrement as fertilizer. You shouldn't eat the fruit.

'Now you've done it.'

'What?'

'Jinxed us. The car's dragging. Can't you hear it?'

Ari wakes up with a start. 'Where are we?'

'Not far from Jericho.'

'Why did you come this way?'

'Not you as well.'

Meyer pulls over to the side of the road and gets out. The front tyre on the driver's side is flat.

'You might as well get out.'

'Why?'

'I have to change the tyre.'

'Can't we stay in?'

'Of course not. I can't jack you up *and* the car.'

The road runs straight ahead flanked by a few half-grown cypresses and emaciated pines. Varda gets out and steps into a pool of shade. In the late afternoon light, the dusty barren fields have taken on a purple-grey hue.

'What time's the wedding?'

'Six.'

'We'll make it. Ari, give me a hand with the jack.'

The boy springs the boot open and removes the jack. Meyer guns the engine. 'You have to do this with a

Citroën. You have to keep the engine running, to get the initial elevation. Now slide the jack under.'

Three small children, all boys, one about ten, the others younger, appear out of nowhere. Meyer thinks: It is always like this. You stare into an empty landscape. There's no one for miles around. Suddenly you're in a crowd. Do they have invisibility cream? Varda would say: You don't want to see them.

The children stand behind Meyer and watch him remove the hubcap. The nuts on the wheel are sticky and hard to get loose. While Meyer works, a jeep appears about a mile down the road, travelling at high speed. When it gets close they can see that it's an army vehicle. There are four soldiers: two in front, and two, with automatic weapons slung round their necks, perched in the back. As they approach, Varda half raises her hand, as if she's about to flag them down. But Meyer gives her a look.

Ari rolls the new tyre over to Meyer and kneels beside him. Varda thinks he looks pleased to be helping. He likes machines, says he wants to be an engineer. Perhaps her sister's new husband will help. He owns a company that manufacturers irrigation pipes, but maybe that isn't really engineering.

'I think this one's flat too.'

'No, it needs air.'

'Do you have a pump?'

'Always prepared.'

Meyer presses on the foot-pump. It's a slow process. Sweat forms on his brow, and starts to run in little streams down the side of his face. His right knee begins to hurt at the joint.

'You try.'

Ari pumps as hard as he can. He gets a little wild, and tries jumping with both feet. The children start to laugh. One of the smaller boys starts to imitate Ari. He leaps up and down until the older boy, speaking with what sounds

like fraternal authority, tells him to stop. Meyer goes over
and inspects the tyre. 'It's no use. There's a hole.'

Varda steps out of the shade. 'Now what?'

Meyer looks around as if a garage is going to materialize
as mysteriously as the three boys. Should he put the flat
back on? Bobble along with the three of them in the car?
How far would they get? He goes over and turns the
engine off. The car sinks down like a wounded bison.

'I'll have to walk into Jericho.'

'What, and leave us here?'

'What else?'

'We can wait for the next car.'

The next car holds four Arab men, and the truck right
behind it, another ten or so. All returning home from
work. By the looks of their equipment they are construction workers, day labourers. Sometimes, when he has
reserve duty, and has to get up very early in the morning,
Meyer sees men like these standing on Jerusalem street
corners, waiting for their bosses to come and pick them
up.

All the men in the car get out, and four or five climb
down from the truck.

Varda walks over to the Citroën, opens the driver's side
door, and slides in behind the wheel. She snaps open
the glove compartment, and starts to rifle through some
papers. Meyer knows she is only pretending to look for
something. He looks back at the sun sinking behind the
Judean hills. When darkness comes it will slam down like
a shutter.

A young man in plaster-covered blue jeans and a lime-
green nylon shirt approaches Meyer. 'Where are you
from?'

'Jerusalem.'

'Where are you going?'

'Tiberias.' Meyer pauses, and then adds, in a friendly
voice, 'We're on our way to a wedding.' Immediately, he
feels ashamed. He is trying to curry favour (who would

do harm to someone on their way to a wedding?), also, and worse, he has heard himself stressing his American accent. He knows that he is trying to disassociate himself, to say, I am not really here, or, if I am, I am not who you think I am. I am not your enemy.

Emboldened by the presence of the others, the three small boys have stuck their heads through the passenger-side window. They are pointing at the lever that raises and lowers the chassis of the car. Varda tells them to go away. She is a school teacher and used to handling inquisitive kids. All the same, she glances around her nervously. She wants to see how the men are reacting to her treatment of the children.

Meyer walks to the edge of the road and looks up and down. The young man in the green shirt follows him. 'Give me the tyres.'

'That's okay. We'll wait.' Meyer means: We'll wait for a car with Jews.

A few steps away Ari has picked up a handful of pebbles and begun throwing them at a telegraph pole. Two more workers descend from the truck. They are younger than the others. Meyer thinks: They should be in school, but nobody cares. The government doesn't care. Their parents don't care. Their bosses certainly don't care.

The boys wander over to Ari and stand near him. Meyer walks over to the car and bends close over Varda, so no one can see what he is saying. 'What do you think?'

'What do I think? I think we could have been in Haifa by now.'

She feels ridiculous in her wedding outfit. Terribly over-dressed. Her sheer, tight blouse. Why did she wear it? To look sexy at her sister's wedding? She should have worn the long dress. If she gets out of the car now, they will all stare at her.

Meyer lifts his head. In the distance, a thin moon has risen over Jericho. When they turned off the main road, Varda had said, in her teacherly way, 'It's the oldest city in the world, seven thousand years. Older than the city of Ur.' He takes two steps away from the car. A hundred yards into the darkness a figure is moving with what appear to be two huge, round, black hands dangling from his arms. Meyer shouts 'Hey!' The figure breaks into a trot. The youth in the lime-green shirt is at his shoulder.

'What's the problem?'

'Where's he going with those tyres?'

Meyer runs twenty yards in pursuit, shouts 'Hey!' again, then stops. He has to return, he can't leave Varda and Ari alone.

One of the older men, a short, stocky individual with thinning hair and a bushy moustache, walks over to inspect the car. He runs his finger down the bonnet, opening a narrow channel in the dust. Varda takes out her pocket mirror, runs a hand through her hair, then erases a smudge of lipstick next to her upper lip. The man looks at her, then turns his attention to Meyer. 'How much?'

'What?'

'How much did you pay for the car?'

More men crowd round. Meyer scans the road for approaching traffic. The questions come in small bursts. 'What's your job?' 'It's a Citroën, yes?' 'You live in Jerusalem? Where?' 'How much?' 'This is your son?'

To this last query Meyer answers 'No,' and then regrets that he has done so. He shouldn't have indicated the possibilities of division. He feels, he doesn't know why, that it is important that Ari and Varda be understood to belong to him. He wants the three of them to be seen as a unit. When the next personal question comes, he lies.

'She is your wife?'

'Yes.'

In order to shake off his interrogators Meyer goes and stands in the middle of the road. He keeps telling himself: Everything's okay, it's not a bad atmosphere, they're only curious, it's okay. He wanders twenty yards down the road, then comes to a halt. It's as if he were on an invisible leash.

There's a commotion under the cypress trees a way off to his right. Varda is out of the car. He hears her shouting, 'Stop! Stop that.' Meyer sprints over. Ari is getting up from the ground, dusting himself off.

'What happened? What happened here?'

One of the Palestinians, judging by his looks the oldest man in the group, is shouting at the two youths. Varda is checking Ari's face, smoothing his hair back to see if his forehead is cut or bruised.

'They pushed Ari down.'

'What did they do to you?'

'Nothing. Spitting.'

'Did they say something? Ari, what did they say to you?'

'What does it matter?'

'Did they . . . ? Did you . . . ?'

'They've got knives. Do you think they don't have knives?'

Meyer turns, his face flushed and angry. The older man is still yelling at the boys, and slowly shoving them away, pressing one of his hands on each of their skinny chests. The boys look insolently over his shoulder, and submit to the pushes a few inches at a time.

When they have moved far enough away, Ari, who is shaking, takes Meyer by the arm. 'Do you have a gun in the car?'

'Why?'

Ari smiles to himself.

'Oh, you're going to shoot. A big shot? You want to shoot someone. You want to shoot those boys?' Meyer feels like slapping Ari across the face. He knows though that it's his own stupidity and impotence that is making him angry. He should have brought a gun.

'You don't have a gun, do you? You drive this way, and you don't carry a gun.'

'I don't need a gun.'

'My father always keeps a gun in his car.'

'I'm not your father.'

Varda comes and lays a hand on Ari's arm. The boy shakes it off. She says, 'The old man gave them a real tongue-lashing.'

Meyer thinks: If I had the gun they would take it from me. They would see me make a move, and they would overwhelm me.

Varda is out now. She feels exposed. She watches green shirt come up to Meyer and ask for a cigarette. She thinks he's come to stare at her breasts. She folds her arms over her chest. If she goes back into the car now it will be obvious that she's scared. But she *is* scared. In any case, she can't leave Ari. He's trying to be tough, but he's fifteen. Why, oh why, didn't they go the other way? In Tiberias, her sister will be under the huppah. She told her not to have a big party. She said, 'For a second marriage, you don't need it.' She had offered to do something small, for family and friends, at *her* apartment. Why did Nurit let the husband arrange the party? Because he was rich? They could all be in Jerusalem now.

Meyer locates a small, wavering light, approaching down the road from off in the distance. A motorbike? Too slow. He looks at the men; they are gathered in small groups, smoking and chatting. Why are they all still here? What are they waiting for? As if in answer, one of the Palestinians starts the engine on the truck. Most of the men, and the three children, start to clamber up behind. The four from the lead car remain, along with the two youths who fought with Ari. As the truck pulls out the old man leans over the side and gestures at the youths. He seems to be admonishing them, but then he starts to laugh, and so do they.

Green shirt introduces himself. He says his name is Samih. Samih is tall and skinny. He wears a black-and-

white chequered scarf around his neck. Has he been wearing that all along, or did he just put it on? 'Your wife?'

'Yes.'

'You have children?'

Meyer doesn't reply.

Samih rubs his two index fingers together, and smiles.
Meyer pretends he hasn't noticed the gesture.

'You need hard work.'

Samih brings his stick fingers under Meyer's face, and
rubs again, trying to light a sexual fire. 'You need very
hard work.'

Meyer looks around to find Varda. She and Ari are
leaning against the car. Soon, someone must come soon.

'You are American?'

Meyer hesitates a moment, then says, 'I was.'

'How long? How long are you in this country?'

'Four years.' This is another lie. And again, Meyer feels
a pang of guilt. He has been in Israel almost ten years. He
thinks: Varda's family goes back five generations. Should I
add that? Why don't I add that?

It's the opposite of what he's trying to say.

Varda comes halfway over from the car. She doesn't
want to talk in front of Samih. Meyer steps towards her.
'What?'

'I have to go to the bathroom.'

'There is no bathroom.'

'You know what I mean.'

'So go.' Meyer doesn't mean to sound so aggressive,
but Samih's finger gesture has unnerved him.

Varda walks off beyond the line of trees towards the
desert. In the dim moonlight she can make out a few
spiny shrubs and the flat top of a lone acacia. She squats
down and lifts her skirt. All the time, she is listening for
sounds of cars, or sounds of scuffle. She rises to go back,
she has peed a little on her skirt (didn't really want to lift
it) and as she starts to walk she can feel the damp hem
touching the back of her legs. There are footsteps, then

laughter, coming out of the semi-darkness. Has she been followed, watched? The crescent moon comes out from behind a cloud and, briefly, casts a silver sheen over the scrubland. Two of the men, out in the desert for the same reason as her, are standing beneath the acacia arching streams of urine into the yellow-brown sand. One of them whistles in her direction. The other shouts something in Arabic. Varda walks straight ahead, picking up her pace. The translation comes: 'Look out for snakes, especially big ones!' Then more laughter. She hears them zip up their pants.

The faltering, pencil-thin light on the road is less than two hundred yards away. Meyer sees that it emanates from the front of a bicycle. The boy pedalling is having a hard time. The passenger perched behind him has a heavy black tyre slung over each of his shoulders.

This time, Ari doesn't help when Meyer puts on the wheel. He stands sullenly, and watches. Samih moves over to his companions. As Meyer adjusts the tyre he can hear them talking and laughing. He calls out to them: 'How much? What do I owe you?'

'Free.'

'No. I want to pay you.'

'Pay what you want to pay.'

Varda thinks: It's over. They are not going to do anything. It's over. In a wave of gratitude she recalls when she used to visit Jericho, when she was in her twenties, years before the intifada. She and a group of friends would drive down from Jerusalem in February, or March, when it was still too cold there to sit outside. In Jericho, they would find a restaurant, one of those off the main street, with blue-tiled fountains, and a fruit stall outside selling blood oranges. The waiters all wore crimson blazers. What was it she had eaten for the first time? Oh, yes. Wood pigeon. In one place there was a boy working in the gardens. Very handsome. She joked about him with her friends. One of the boys in her group, Uri, said to her, 'Six months on a desert island, him or me?' And, not only to teach him a lesson, but also because she felt, at that moment, that she meant it, she said, 'Him.' Uri got very angry. He knocked something off the table, and called the boy over to sweep it up. The other friends were embarrassed. She told Uri that he disgusted her.

Meyer tells her to move out of the way. He gets in and turns the key in the ignition. The car bucks and rises. Ari gets in the back seat and slams the door. Varda moves around to the passenger side. As she does so Samih and his friends approach the car. One of them brushes past her. Too close? She gets in the car. Meyer could put his foot on the gas. They could be gone.

Meyer stretches an arm out of the window and offers a banknote. Samih takes it; he says, 'No problem.'

Meyer replies by echoing him, 'No problem,' and releases the emergency brake.

The two teenage boys have their faces and hands pressed up against the back window; their noses are flattened and distorted. Ari tries to avoid them by looking straight ahead. When the car starts to move they begin to bang hard on the window, and on the roof. The car stalls. The beating on the windows and roof gets harder and harder. A man has joined the boys, he's banging with a stone at Varda's window. The glass splinters into a spider's web, one more blow and he'll be through. Varda bends her head into her hands. Meyer starts the engine. Ari leans forward and screams at him, 'Don't stop.'

FOR THE BEST IN PAPERBACKS, LOOK FOR THE

In every corner of the world, on every subject under the sun, Penguin represents quality and variety—the very best in publishing today.

For complete information about books available from Penguin—including Puffins, Penguin Classics, and Arkana—and how to order them, write to us at the appropriate address below. Please note that for copyright reasons the selection of books varies from country to country.

In the United Kingdom: Please write to *Dept. JC, Penguin Books Ltd, FREEPOST, West Drayton, Middlesex UB7 0BR.*

If you have any difficulty in obtaining a title, please send your order with the correct money, plus ten percent for postage and packaging, to *P.O. Box No. 11, West Drayton, Middlesex UB7 0BR*

In the United States: Please write to *Consumer Sales, Penguin USA, P.O. Box 999, Dept. 17109, Bergenfield, New Jersey 07621-0120.* Visa and MasterCard holders call 1-800-253-6476 to order all Penguin titles

In Canada: Please write to *Penguin Books Canada Ltd, 10 Alcorn Avenue, Suite 300, Toronto, Ontario M4V 3B2*

In Australia: Please write to *Penguin Books Australia Ltd, P.O. Box 257, Ringwood, Victoria 3134*

In New Zealand: Please write to *Penguin Books (NZ) Ltd, Private Bag 102902, North Shore Mail Centre, Auckland 10*

In India: Please write to *Penguin Books India Pvt Ltd, 706 Eros Apartments, 56 Nehru Place, New Delhi 110 019*

In the Netherlands: Please write to *Penguin Books Netherlands bv, Postbus 3507, NL-1001 AH Amsterdam*

In Germany: Please write to *Penguin Books Deutschland GmbH, Metzlerstrasse 26, 60594 Frankfurt am Main*

In Spain: Please write to *Penguin Books S. A., Bravo Murillo 19, 1° B, 28015 Madrid*

In Italy: Please write to *Penguin Italia s.r.l., Via Felice Casati 20, I-20124 Milano*

In France: Please write to *Penguin France S. A., 17 rue Lejeune, F–31000 Toulouse*

In Japan: Please write to *Penguin Books Japan, Ishikiribashi Building, 2–5–4, Suido, Bunkyo-ku, Tokyo 112*

In Greece: Please write to *Penguin Hellas Ltd, Dimocritou 3, GR–106 71 Athens*

In South Africa: Please write to *Longman Penguin Southern Africa (Pty) Ltd, Private Bag X08, Bertsham 2013*